Harry Hazelton

Quindaro

Or, the heroine of Fort Laramie. A tale of the far West.

Harry Hazelton

Quindaro
Or, the heroine of Fort Laramie. A tale of the far West.

ISBN/EAN: 9783337214050

Printed in Europe, USA, Canada, Australia, Japan

Cover: Foto ©Andreas Hilbeck / pixelio.de

More available books at **www.hansebooks.com**

OR,

THE HEROINE OF FORT LARAMIE.

A Tale of the Far West.

BY

THE AUTHOR OF "THE SILVER BUGLE."

LONDON AND NEW YORK

GEORGE ROUTLEDGE AND SONS.

QUINDARO.

CHAPTER I.

FORT LARAMIE AND ITS HEROINE.

THE sun never shone upon a spot more wildly beautiful in its variety than the plains of Laramie. To one who has never visited western Nebraska, it may appear singular that the name *plains* should be applied to a portion of country in the very midst of the most prominent peaks and ridges of the Rocky mountains. But, in spite of their location, the title is far from being inappropriate. Fort Laramie is situated at the junction of the north fork of the Nebraska or Platte river, and one of lesser note, bearing its own name. The Platte river, from this point to its source, describes nearly a circle, winding through the mountains for a distance of four hundred miles. Laramie river rises but a few miles from the head of the Platte, but, running in an almost direct course, thus quite completes the circle, forming an inclosure of about seventy-five miles in extent. Within this inclosure are the celebrated *Laramie plains.* It is not simply a wide-spreading prairie, but a series of valleys, varying in size, nestling at the base of lofty ridges. Through these valleys flow innumerable small streams. They appear to rise from one common center, and, diverging, empty their clear waters into the Platte or Laramie.

And the mountains here, in their grandeur, present a striking contrast to the peaceful beauty of the vales below. "Laramie Peak" is perhaps the most prominent. It is about twenty miles from the fort which bears its name. From its most elevated point, a magnificent view of the rolling prairies, stretching toward the Missouri, can be had; also, of the valley of the Platte, the river itself, and the narrow strips of woodland which, at intervals, fringe its banks.

To the westward, the view is different. Far as the eye can reach, are the ragged mountain tops, amid which are t places of interest, to which especial reference must be made. These are known as "Rock Independence," and "Devil's Gate." The former is an elevated peak, nearly barren of verdure, perhaps four thousand feet in hight. At its summit is a huge rock bearing the name indicated. It appears to have formed the termination of an immense ridge, but had become isolated, in order to give free course to the Sweetwater river, which flows through a narrow opening, bearing the suggestive title of the "Devil's Gate." Indeed, the river passes *under* "Independence Rock," and the name "Devil's Gate" is suggested from the surrounding gloom, the roaring waters, and the huge caverns formed in the mountain's side.

The period of which we write was the year 1857–8. At that time, Fort Kearney, about two hundred miles from the Missouri border, was the extreme western settlement. It is true that many adventuresome and daring spirits had advanced far into the interior, and many a squatter's cabin dotted the valley of the Platte, even to the base of the mountain ridges; but the intervals between these were often many miles in extent, and the country could not be called *settled*.

Now it is fair to suppose that the term "squatter" implies the roughest and most unlettered backwoodsman. As a general rule, this is the case. But, as there are exceptions to all rules, so there were exceptions in this case; and the plains of Nebraska could boast a few families of refinement, who had been induced by reverse of fortune, or some like repellent cause, to seek a home "far from the haunts of men," amid the sublime solitudes of those western valleys, where the buffalo and the Indian still roamed in their aboriginal freedom.

Fort Laramie, at that time, was of considerable importance as a trading-post with the Indians, and was usually occupied by about three hundred United States troops. It was also of importance as a protection to trains destined for the Golden State, which chose the route *via* Platte valley, the Sweetwater, South Pass and Fort Hall.

There was, perhaps, a half-dozen cabins beyond the first link of mountains, and spread over Laramie plains at intervals varying from five to twenty miles. To one of these lonely habitations we direct the reader's attention. Though by no means remarkable in appearance it was decidedly so in situation

It was located near the junction of the Platte and Medicine Bow rivers, and about five miles from the mouth of the Sweetwater, or fifteen from Devil's Gate. The peculiar feature connected with the cabin was, that, instead of having been erected in the valley, which was one of the most lovely in the plains, it stood about one hundred feet up the sharp mountain side, and was almost entirely concealed from view by the foliage and the ragged rocks. Indeed, the passage from the base of the mountain up to the cabin, was a thing not easily accomplished, unless by one familiar with the spot.

When the traveler, leaving civilization, penetrates the western wilds, he is apt to feel a sense of utter loneliness, even though accompanied by congenial companions. Before him rolls the vast prairie, or the dense forest greets his vision. The buffalo, the wild horse, the prairie-wolf, the deer and the roaming savage, become objects familiar to him, and he longs for those scenes he has so recently left.

So when Fort Laramie, with its civilization, is approached by the adventurer, after a journey of four hundred miles through the barren wastes of Nebraska, no wonder the sight is a welcome one.

Nor was the most attractive feature of the fort the presence of its officers, its soldiers and their families. There was a "heroine" present, around whom centered much of interest and romance. Her story is as follows:

Manonie, or Wild Bird, as she was called by the savages, was a "pale-face." Of her parentage, nothing was known, excepting by the chief of the Pawnees, Nemona, or "Rushing Waters." The father of Nemona had captured the girl in central Iowa, when she was but three years of age. The fate of her parents was unknown. Manonie herself was ignorant of the fact of her being of white blood, until by chance she learned it from one of the officers of Laramie, with whom she had become acquainted, and who had gleaned this much of her history from an Indian, by bribe and cajolery.

Manonie, or Wild Bird, as she was commonly called, had considerable affection for her dusky friends, for, in truth, she had been treated with especial kindness by them, or rather by the chief. There was, however, a brave called Wontum, or Wild Cat, who had sought the maid in marriage, but had been spurned. It appeared as if the proud nature of one nobly born had been suddenly aroused within her, when thus solicited; for there was such an exhibition of indignation and disgust that even Wontum slunk away in shame or fear.

Nemona, the chief, as is quite unusual with the savage, had a wife to whom he was truly attached, and cared not to take a second. He therefore attempted to use his influence with his beautiful foster-sister in favor of Wontum; but, to no purpose. Indeed, it resulted in high words and no little bitterness of feeling between the maid and the chief; and so, Manonie was left to herself. Wontum, ascertaining this fact, lost no opportunity to urge his suit, and also to use threats, to all of which the maiden returned her first scornful reply.

However, from that moment she began to absent herself much from the Indian villages; while, from her excessive caution when she found herself liable to encounter her persecutor, she received the title of "Wild Bird." The maiden was, at that time, about fifteen years of age. During the year following the proposal and rejection, she often visited the few white settlers then residing on the plains. Her distaste for the savage life appeared to grow upon her; her "white" instincts began to assert themselves.

At length she met a young lieutenant from the fort, who had heard her story, or a portion of it, from the settlers. He became her willing tutor. She was a ready pupil. At first he felt an interest, then a sympathy, and, finally, found himself deeply in love. Nor was it a hopeless passion, for it was returned with all the ardor of an impulsive soul. The young man discovered in the beautiful girl a nature of singular purity, an intellect of remarkable quickness, and a grace as exquisite as if the dancing waters had been her tutor. It would have been strange if Henry Marshall, a lieutenant in the United States army, of proud family and independent spirit, had not loved the unknown forest-maiden, for few hearts could have passed the ordeal of her eyes and tongue and not have dreamed of Houris and their enchantments.

The engagement between the lovers soon became known throughout the tribe, and a bitter feeling was engendered in consequence. The chief, it is true, gave little heed to the matter, but Wontum declared at once for a savage vengeance.

Influential with the tribe, a large number consented to join him in any thing he might attempt, to secure his prize and to thwart the proud pale-face. The maiden was, soon thereafter, made a prisoner in the village, but succeeded in escaping, and reached the fort in safety.

Chagrined and furious at the girl's desertion of her tribe, Wontum formed a plan for her recapture. He attacked a train at " South Pass," but, instead of killing the emigrants, he made them prisoners. By design, however, he let one of the party escape, who made his way directly to Laramie, with the intelligence of the attack and capture. This was as the wily savage designed—his purpose being to draw as many of the troops away from the fort as possible, in his pursuit, thus to leave it weak enough for the consummation of his further diabolical strategy.

He conveyed his plunder and prisoners to the very summit of " Table Hill," which adjoins the Pass. This is, perhaps, one of the most formidable peaks of the Rocky ranges. It is very steep, ragged, thickly timbered, and is seven thousand four hundred and eighty-eight feet in hight—a truly formidable landmark even among its rugged brothers.

It was not the purpose of Wontum to remain at Table Hill with his entire force, which consisted of about two hundred warriors. He left, at the hill, about twenty of his painted cut-throats, and, with the remainder, set out for the fort, which he intended to surprise, and, after having destroyed the garrison, to seize Manonie and make his escape.

The distance from South Pass to Laramie was nearly two hundred miles. Perhaps half the distance had been passed, when the savages saw the approaching troops. They concealed themselves until all danger of an encounter was over, and then pressed rapidly forward. The strategist's plans appeared to work well.

There had been left at the fort a force of about forty men— Lieutenant Henry Marshall being in command. The marriage ceremony with his forest-queen had not yet taken place, although Manonie remained within the post—a guest and pupil of the officers' ladies. The attack upon the emigrants convinced her that Wontum was on the war-path, and her forest instincts at once were on the alert. What was the ultimate *design* of the chief? She feared even for her safety in the fort, and conceived that the attack had in it some design on her and her now very dear friends. Silently she withdrew from the fortification, and at once passed off into the valley above, determined to watch, with her keen eye, for any sign of coming disaster. All day long was she absent, until Marshall became exceedingly uneasy at her stay. Just as darkness settled over all, her light form came into view from the sallyport, and she was admitted, evidently weary from a long day's journey. She had seen sufficient to convince her that a large party of savages were approaching, and the little garrison at once made preparation for a defense.

The assault was made at midnight, and the savages, not anticipating so warm a reception, fell back in disorder. A regular siege was then commenced, and all the arts and devices known to those tigers of the plains, were employed by Wontum, to carry out his scheme of murder and seizure. The third day of the siege arrived. Lieutenant Marshall had been wounded, and the men, weary with watching, and left without a commander, gave evidence of yielding.

It was about midnight of the third day, that the Indians made a most desperate charge. They were received with less determination than before. Encouraged by this, several of the most daring, led by Wontum, sprung within the inclosure. Manonie was then seated beside the bed of her wounded lover, but at this crisis she sprung forward, and, seizing a sword, fought with the fury of desperation, while she called upon those around to imitate her example. The result was that the savages were again repulsed with fearful loss, for, inspired by her astonishing bravery, the troops, with a wild huzza, rushed into the hand-to-hand conflict, and the fort was saved.

Wontum, finding it impossible to secure the maid, surrounded as she was by the soldiers, sought out Marshall. His bloody knife gleamed in the dim light, and was about to become warm with the blood of the wounded man, when Manonie appeared and leveled a terrible blow at the head of the savage. Her aim, in consequence of her intense excitement, was not altogether true, but the sharp steel fell upon the uplifted arm, and Wontum, with a yell of pain and rage, sprang from the room and made his escape. The siege was ended, as the troops returned the following morning, and the savage retired to his mountain lairs to await another opportunity for striking the fatal blow.

So Manonie, the Wild Bird, became the "heroine of Fort Laramie." And shortly after there was a marriage celebration, and the forest-beauty became the happy wife of Henry Marshall. Then a year passed—a dear, delicious year, so full of sweets and wild delights as to make earth a paradise—and she became a mother. Another, and another rolled around, and little Harry Marshall became the pet of the fort.

The "heroine" was not forgotten. Her fame had spread far across the prairies, and when the traveler arrived at that outpost of civilization, almost the first inquiry was for its brave and beautiful defender.

Every effort had been made to ascertain the parentage of the now wife and mother, but without success. Many fathers, whose little ones had been stolen from them years before, visited the fort, but failed to recognize any feature, or fact, which could identify her as their own. As for herself, the recollection of her early home dawned slowly but indistinctly upon her. One by one, incidents and acts of her early life came back to her; scenes and forms took shape, until, out of that mist of distance, her childhood's home arose clearly and distinctly, and she declared that she would be able to recognize her father if she should meet him, unless, indeed, he had changed very much since her infancy. With her advance in education and refinement, her desire to ascertain the secret of her birth, and to find her parents, became daily greater. Not that she was unquiet or over-eager in her truly blissful wife's estate; but, the affection which holy nature has implanted in our hearts for the authors of our being, welled up in her own, and, day and night, her prayer went up for the lost but loved ones who knew her not.

At the time our story opens, Lieutenant Marshall and his wife were still at Fort Laramie, although they were about to take their departure for Leavenworth. They had been three years married, and little Harry, their only-born, the idol of his parents, and of all the troops stationed at Laramie, was two years of age.

CHAPTER II.

OLD JOHN.

WE referred to the cabin situated at the junction of the Platte and Medicine Bow rivers, up the hill-side, so hidden away, like some eagle's nest, that even the lynx-eye of the savage might not detect it.

It was scarcely light, on the morning of the 20th of September, in the year 1857. A young man, mounted upon a splendid animal, approached the base of the hill, or rather ledge, where stood the lonely cabin. He had been attracted toward the spot by the smoke which curled up among the trees. He soon found it impossible to proceed, on account of the broken rocks, and, dismounting, bent his course upward. As he clambered along, he exclaimed :

" This hermit must possess a taste decidedly romantic, or he never would have selected such a spot for his dwelling. His name is not quite romantic enough for the location of his cabin. Old John is commonplace, surely. Yet he is a strange man. I can learn nothing about him of the settlers upon the plains." These words were spoken as if addressed to some companion, although none was near.

The speaker had reached a little open space, upon which the cabin stood, as this self-colloquy was ended.

" What do you wish to learn of him?" asked a voice close by his side. The young man gazed upon the speaker with some degree of interest not unmingled with astonishment. He was a man of powerful frame. His eyes were sunken and almost concealed beneath the shaggy brows, while the long, white locks of hair hung about his shoulders, straggling and wild. His beard was of the same hue, and was in perfect keeping with other portions of his " get-up." His voice was low, but firm and commanding, and was not untinged with melancholy. The young man did not reply for several moments. The cause of his silence he scarcely realized himself. The old man, observing his hesitation, said :

" You left too fine an animal at the foot of the ledge. Did you want it to fall into the hands of the *legyos* ?"

" I don't understand you."

" Oh !—legyos ?—you don't know its meaning ?"

" No. It is a name or title which I have never before heard ; nor do I understand its significance. But I confess I would not like any misfortune to befall Dahlgren."

" Oh, yes ; I see. That is the name of your horse. Well, here he is." The young man turned, and saw his steed feeding, in a quiet manner, between two huge rocks, which formed a perfect shelter. He sprung forward, and, ascertaining that it was indeed his own beast, asked :

" How did you bring him so quickly to this point ? It can not be more than twenty minutes since I left him securely fastened to a tree below."

" Yes. And in five minutes after you left him, he would have been in the hands of the legyos."

" The legyos again."

" Yes. It is the Indian name for assassin—for midnight murderers."

" And they would have seized my horse ?"

" Yes. Did you expect less ?"

" Not if any of the savages were near me. But, I thought my journey across the valley was unobserved by them."

" You must pardon me, young man, but you are a fool."

" You must pardon *me*, sir. But I am not accustomed to be addressed by such a title, nor will I permit it."

" You prefer to do as you please, I suppose ?"

" Not so, sir. If I can deem you my friend, I will take your advice. Still I confess I do not accept the title you gave me."

" Well, then, I ask your pardon. But you know old age is privileged."

" You have done me a favor, sir ; and, therefore, you may claim a free pardon."

" Why are you here alone ?" asked the old man, as he fixed his gaze upon his visitor. " It is not safe for a person to travel singly through these valleys, more especially if he is well mounted and wears the uniform of the United States army."

"It is not my choice. I have—pardon me, sir; but are you not the person known as John, the hermit?"

The old man bowed his head, and, for some time, remained silent. There was a slight tremor visible, and a half-suppressed moan. The young man gazed upon the hermit with an interest not unmingled with sympathy. He felt that some heavy grief must be his or he never would have thus isolated himself from mankind. But what that grief might be the young officer had not the slightest intimation, and he considerately refrained from asking any questions lest it might be the cause of opening afresh some terrible wound. He had heard much of Old John, the hermit, as a strange but peaceable man, who was feared by the savages—a fear caused by superstition. They believed him possessed of supernatural powers, and never approached nearer his cabin than the base of the cliff. It could scarcely be that his sorrow was the result of any savage barbarity, as he had never been known to interfere, in the slightest manner, with any of the red-men. More than this, some of the settlers in the valley declared that the *solitaire* was decidedly pious, as he had often been found praying when they had visited him. But such visits were rare. It had, therefore, been decided, that his grief must have some connection with his former life, and that he had voluntarily exiled himself from scenes where he could no longer be happy.

At length the old man raised his head, and, to the question replied:

"Yes. I am the old hermit, as I am usually called by those who know little of me. Still, I am not a hermit, or recluse, as you infer."

The young man gazed around expecting to see others who were sharing that solitude. The old man observed this, and continued:

"No wife or children greet me here, I grant you. And yet, I am not alone. Gaze around you. What do you see?"

"Very little but gloom. True, there is a valley below; and it has much claim to natural beauty; but, then, it is so monotonous—ever the same. And that river glitters in the morning sun; but its brightness wearies the eye at length, and it never changes."

"No. It is like its Creator—it never changes. Well it is

that it is ever the same. You are fond of change. Look upon me. I was once young as yourself; but I *have* changed. And my life has changed more than my person. You are happy now. Do you wish change to come to you, and bring you misery? Oh, beware how you become discontented with blessings the Almighty has encircled you with. Listen to the warbling of these birds. They are always happy, and *they* change not. Listen to that gushing rill. Its music never ceases. Look at the silver of that water-spring. See how the bubbling liquid is rolling up from the bright sands at its bottom. I have quenched my thirst there a thousand times. And it has not changed for six long years. Should you wish for change in that? Oh, may the day never come to you, that you will pray for things as they *were* and not as they *are.*"

"You are painting a very gloomy picture for a young life. That is, you are supposing if change comes it must be for the worse. May it not, in some instances, be for the better? We will take your own case, for example. Could nothing occur to render you happier than you are?"

"Yes; I think so. Do you recollect the last remarkable words which were spoken by the dying Baron Humboldt?"

"I can not say that I do."

"I will tell you. The good old man was closing up a life of usefulness. Through the closed blinds of his room a sun-ray stole and danced upon the ceiling. He gazed upon it a moment, and then exclaimed:

"'Oh! how beautiful! Oh! how beautiful!'

"He had seen that sunbeam ten thousand times, and had never longed for a change in it. It was as lovely to him as it ever had been. But now the time for change had come for him and that sunbeam, and he continued:

"'Oh! how beautiful! *It seems to beckon earth to heaven!'*

"And so, young man, when *that* change comes for me, it will be a welcome one. But you did not tell me how you came to be here alone, and who you are, although I suppose you came from the fort."

"I am Lieutenant Henry Marshall."

"Ah, yes! I remember having seen you as you passed up the valley some ten days since; but you were so far distant,

at that time, that I did not recognize you at once to-day
Where are your men ?"

"Not one of them lives."

"Indeed !"

"Yes ; we were surprised, near the South Pass, by a party
of savages, and I alone escaped, to bear the sad tidings to the
fort. It was a sad work, sir—a sad work !" and the young
officer sighed heavily over his lost companions.

"What tribe did the attacking party belong to ?"

"I do not know. I should judge they were the Pawnees.
Wontum, one of their braves, has sworn to take my life, and,
if possible, to capture my wife and child. But I did not see
him with the savages who assailed us, though he *may* have
been their director."

"No. He passed down the valley, toward Laramie, three
days since."

"Is it possible ! Was he alone ?" asked Marshall, with some
excitement.

"No. His warriors were with him—all in war-paint, and
athirst for blood."

"How large a number ?"

"Not less than three hundred."

"And in war-paint, too," he mused. "Are you sure Wontum led them in person ?"

"I can not answer positively, as the distance between us was
so great. But they were in war-costume, and, for several
reasons, I believe them to have been Wontum's band."

Marshall sighed heavily, and grew pale ; but quickly the
blood mounted to his face, as he pressed his hands to his
brow. The old man observing this, asked :

"Do you believe they really intend to attack the fort ?"

"Yes ; and I tremble for the consequences. The garrison
is not strong."

"But will no doubt be able to defend it. If I am not mistaken, your fears are more directly connected with the settlers
than the soldiers."

"I don't know that I have any especial fears with regard
to either. But when I am absent, of late, there is a weight
upon my heart which I can not explain. I do believe that I
have become a coward on account of my wife and child."

"Are they not safe in the fort?"

"Yes; I believe they are secure there. It is not because my judgment tells me that they are in any danger, but a presentiment oppresses me. If harm should come to them, it would kill me."

"Guard them well, young man. They are treasures that, once lost, can never be regained," added the old man fervently, as a tear trembled upon his eyelid.

"Ay, guard them well I will. I must be away at once. I came here for concealment while my poor animal gained a little rest. But every moment is precious."

"There is great danger between this place and the fort. The valley is full of the bloodthirsty wretches."

"Still I must venture the journey. Were the path infested every rod with rattlesnakes, I should press on."

"That is nobly spoken. I honor your devotion. But you must not—shall not, go alone."

"Who will go with me? Who would share such peril?"

"I will."

"What! Leave your fastness here where you are so secure in your isolation?"

"I am not so much of a *solitaire* as you suppose. I devote much of my time to assisting the unfortunate wayfarer and settler. You must not pass through the valley. I will be your guide over the mountains, as that is the only feasible route now."

"And I'll go along, as sure as my name's Jack Oakley," added a speaker, who came up at that moment. The hermit extending his hand in welcome to the new-comer asked:

"Do you bring any thing of importance?"

"Wal, rather 'portant to me."

"What is it?" asked old John.

"Oh, jes' about the old sort. Brought up Molly, the baby and the old woman. Want to let 'em be here a bit."

"Then there must be some trouble if you bring your family here for safety. But, they are welcome, as they always have been."

"I knew they would be. And they'll be all safe here, fo the legyos would as soon think of facin' Old Nick in his owi regions, as coming up here."

The parties spoken of made their appearance, and entered the cabin—two females and a babe.

"Have you any special news?" asked the hermit.

"Nothin' further than that about two hundred of the red-skins have gone down the Platte, and that lots on 'em are sneakin' about. I think our best way is to go straight across the mountains, and down the Laramie river. That's the clearest way, I reck'n, jist now, and, shouldn't wonder a bit cf we come across some of the villains, even in the hills."

The preparations were soon made, and the party, consist-ing of Marshall, old John, and Oakley, set out for the fort. Of course, Dahlgren, the horse, was not left behind.

CHAPTER III

WONTUM AND HIS VICTIMS.

THE savages had received a severe punishment for their attack upon the fort and the train. The lesson was a whole-some one, and, for the three years after the marriage of Lieutenant Marshall and Manonie, the Pawnees had commit-ted very few depredations. Most of those which were com-mitted resulted from the direct influence of Wontum, whose savage hatred of the whites abated not, but rather grew in intensity—especially toward the man who had won the heart of the beautiful " Wild Bird." How to glut his fiendish pas-sion for revenge became his sole study. All the brute instinct of his nature was aroused. His heart was on fire with fever for the moment when he could strike. How to strike and give the worst pain was his frequent subject of meditation. To slay was but an ordinary expression of hate. A scalp-lock more or less did not matter. To agonize, to torture, was his only purpose. Such a creature is the American Indian when once his *true nature* is permitted full sway. All the fables of ancient ferocity are shown in the reality of his life when the hatchet is dug up and the war-paint is on. Christian sentiments lay upon his mind only as leaves to be blown away by the first tempest. The "civilized" Pawnee, or Sioux, or Crow, is just as much civilized as one of Herr Driesbach's tigers—no more. The thirst for blood never dies. His Indian nature may be modified by the momentary influ ences of fear, whisky or want, but give him his own wilds and the hyena is not more cruel—the wolf not more heartless. This is the American aborigine as he is by *nature* and *instinct*— as he will ever be so long as he is an Indian. When the Apache is tamed, or the Comanche is brought under control, the Rocky mountains will have disappeared, and the Valley of Delights will have taken their place.

To give most pain, Wontum had resolved to get possession of Marshall's child, for that would also give him possession of Manonie, who, he well knew, would not hesitate to follow after her offspring—were it even to walk the burning path to the stake. To this end, he commenced depredations in various directions, intending to create a bitter feeling between the soldiers and his tribe, and thus bring on a general war, which the old chief had endeavored to avoid. The bronze-hearted villain had committed a number of murders, which he represented as having been done by the pale-faces, taking care that the victims should belong to the Pawnees, or to some friendly neighboring tribe.

At length Nemona, the head chief, aggravated by these re-peated murders, gave his consent for the commencement of hostilities—so successfully had Wontum manœuvered. The savages took possession of "Devil's Gate," fortifying them-selves upon the rocks adjoining. Their position was a strong one. The first attack was made as usual upon a train. This drew from the fort a small body of men, every one of whom was killed or captured with the exception of Marshall, whom, in the last chapter, we found with the hermit upon his return from the fatal expedition.

After this attack, Wontum made a rapid movement down the Platte, and arrived in the vicinity of the fort long before the result of Marshall's expedition had become known. This was as he wished, as he had resolved to employ stratagem to effect his chief purpose of securing the child and mother. He concealed his warriors in a dense thicket only a short dis-tance from the fort, and under the darkness of a stormy night, advanced for the purpose of reconnoitering the works. He was without his war-dress or paint.

It was not supposed at Fort Laramie that any thing like a general war was intended; nor was there the most remote idea that the fort would be attacked. The guard, therefore, was not as vigilant as in more dangerous times.

Wontum found little difficulty in reaching the outer work, but now the greatest obstacle presented itself. It was after *twelve* o'clock, and the very presence of an Indian, at such an hour of the night, would create suspicion at any time. But now that there were rumors of depredations by the Pawnees, if it should be discovered that one of their number, and that one a brave, was lurking around at such an hour, he would certainly be arrested, and perhaps executed as a spy and marauder. He therefore advanced with extreme caution, until the entrance of the fort was reached. The huge door was closed. Beside it stood a sentinel leaning lazily against the wall, his gun resting by his side. While considering how to act, the door or gate swung back with a heavy sound, and the relief-guard made its appearance. The drowsy sentinel sprung up, and advanced to meet his comrades.

Wontum took advantage of the momentary engagement of the soldiers, and of the heavy darkness, to glide through the open gate. Then he found himself within the coveted inclosure, but upon strange ground. He had been within the fort but once before, and to gain some knowledge of its interior was of much importance to him. Of course he could not know the location of the different sentry-posts, and to move around, no matter with how much caution, involved no small amount of danger. But, that master-passion of his soul, revenge, was stronger than his fear, and he resolved to "do or die."

He heard the massive door reclose, and then the tread of the sentry as they returned to their guard-house. He had no knowledge of camp-life, but his natural instinct was sufficient to teach him that, as in the Indian villages, the better class of buildings would be assigned the officers highest in rank. Before him were a long row of white buildings or barracks, and to the right, at the other entrance, were others, which, from their appearance, he judged to be those he sought. To reach them he would be compelled to cross an open space; but the darkness was so intense, that there would be little danger of detection, if great caution was used.

In the buildings which he intended reaching, there gleamed a faint light in one of the lower windows, and quite a number in those of the second story. Elsewhere all was dark; not a sound broke the stillness of the night, save the pattering of the rain upon the hard-packed walls, and the moaning of the wind. All were at rest, with the exception of those whose duty it was to watch, unless it might be those who were occupying the lighted rooms. And if there was a sleepless eye or aching heart within those walls, why should it not be Manonic, the Wild Bird? Her husband was absent, but not her protectors; for here were those who would have fought in her defense, even unto death. How well he noticed this his silent movements gave evidence. A shadow could not have been more noiseless, nor a serpent more alert. He glided across the open space, crouching close to the ground, ever and anon pausing to listen, and to mark his course. But his progress was uninterrupted, and, at length, he reached the main building. Then he crept close to a window from which gleamed a feeble light. But a thick curtain prevented him seeing what was taking place within. He placed his ear near the glass, and listened. There was no sound to be heard. He tapped lightly upon the pane, and still all was silent.

"Sleep—sleep," he muttered. "This was captain's room long time ago when hurt. Must find if be his room now."

He repeated his blows upon the window; this time with more vigor. In a moment he heard a movement within. He sprung back and prostrated himself closely upon the ground.

Although it was only the month of September, and the days were as warm as midsummer, yet the nights were cool, and, as it was storming, this one was especially unpleasant. The windows of the building were closed in consequence. But the one at which the savage had stationed himself, was now thrown open, and the inmate of the room peered forth into the surrounding gloom. It was difficult to determine whether the form was that of a male or female.

At the same moment another window directly over this one, and from which streamed a bright light, was also thrown up, and a form appeared which was easily recognized as that of a female. Apparently addressing herself to the person below, she asked:

"Did you not hear an unusual sound, Lieutenant Blair?"

"I did, Manonie. Did *you* observe any thing especial?"

"I did. I have not slept, and I have listened attentively, that I might hear the approach of my husband, should he arrive to-night. And I am sure I distinctly heard some person, or some thing, tapping upon your window."

"I think we were both deceived. It must have been the rain, or the rattle of the sash by the wind."

"I think not. I have listened to every sound, and this one only lasted for an instant; and during the whole night it was the only one like it. I should not be at all surprised if there were Indians lurking around."

"Oh, no, Manonie. You are nervous to-night on account of the absence of your husband. It would be impossible for a savage to enter the fort without being discovered. You had better retire. This constant watching will be too much for you."

"It would be useless, for I could not rest. Besides, my little Harry has been wakeful and feverish all the earlier part of the night. But he is sleeping now."

"Probably only the natural anxiety of a mother causes you to fancy this. Come, retire now, and think no more of this. And if the noise is again repeated, I will go for a guard and have a thorough search made."

"You have not heard any thing from my husband and our friends yet, have you?"

"Not yet. But I have no fears for their safety."

"I have. What I have observed for the past few days has led me to believe that the savages mean mischief. I have seen a number of them lurking around, and I think their presence bodes no good. And I think my husband was accompanied by too few of our men.'"

"But we have sent another hundred. We shall probably learn of their safety by to-morrow."

"God grant it. Good-night." Manonie closed her window.

Lieutenant Blair remained a moment more gazing into the darkness, and then dropping the sash, retired. The savage started to his feet. In the dim light which shone through the window, could be seen a truly demoniac expression which lit up his face like a fire from within. His prey was within his grasp! He had learned that the husband of Manonie still was absent, and had discovered the room she occupied. He knew the garrison of the fort had been weakened by the absence of one hundred men, besides the party which had been indiscriminately slaughtered a few days before, at "Devil's Gate." The present number of soldiers could not, then, exceed a hundred. If they could be thoroughly surprised, a victory could be gained! The delighted monster with difficulty restrained the wild *whoop* of satisfaction which trembled upon his lips.

His first impulse was to return to his warriors, and then make the attack. But he was satisfied that daylight would come before he could get every thing in readiness; and to meet the garrison well prepared for defense, would be to run a very great chance of another defeat. But, over and above all, he felt a malicious desire to accomplish *alone* the revenge which his heart had been so long set upon. In an instant he had determined upon his plans. Blair had said that if he heard the noise again, he would *go for a guard.*

The savage again approached the window, and tapped lightly. It was not his purpose to have Manonie hear. This done, he again sprung back. The sash was again thrown up, and Blair called to know who was there. Of course no answer came. The lieutenant then crossed his room and threw open the hall-door. The savage heard his retreating footsteps, and, quick as thought, he sprung through the open window into the vacant room. This done, he concealed himself beneath the bed. Hearing the lieutenant giving directions for a thorough search, he grinned in his devilish glee at the success of his ruse.

It was but a short time before the officer returned to his room, and, seating himself by his table, began the perusal of some papers. An hour passed, and a corporal entered announcing the fact that a thorough search had been made, but nothing unusual had been found. The officer then closed his window and retired to his couch for sleep.

Another hour passed and the heavy breathing of Blair

convinced the savage that he was sleeping. Cautiously he crawled forth, and, seating himself by the bedside, gazed upon his intended and unconscious victim. He drew from his belt a long, sharp knife, and toyed with its point, as if he wished to lengthen, as far as possible, the joy he felt at having one hated foe thus in his power. He arose to his feet and bent over the sleeper. He raised the knife. It glittered in the light; and then he lowered it again. Was it some good angel that held his arm? And was it this which caused the fated man to smile in his sleep? Perhaps it was that his soul was about to be transferred from a world of strife to those bright realms where revenge and hate were words unknown. Lieutenant Blair was truly a Christian soldier, beloved by all with whom he was associated.

At length the sleeper opened his eyes. He attempted to rise, but he felt the sharp point of the knife at his heart.

" No speak loud!" exclaimed the savage.

" What would you?" asked the lieutenant.

" Me kill you—quick—there!"

Poor Blair closed his eyes—groaned—the work was done.

The monster gazed upon the dead man, and, for several moments, remained motionless. At length he turned and walked to the door. He opened it and peered into the hall. A dim light was burning, but all was silent. He stepped cautiously forth, and walked along the passage. It was not long before he found the steps leading to the second floor. These he ascended, pausing before the door of the apartment which was occupied by the mother and child. He listened : not a sound was heard. But through a crevice he could see that a light still was burning. He touched the latch, but found the door fast. Here was a dilemma. What was to be done? If he attempted to force it, she would be aroused even if she was then asleep, and would give the alarm.

Satan sometimes appears to assist his own in a wonderful manner, when they are engaged in doing his work. So it appeared on this occasion.

At this moment the heavy tread of the " rounds" was heard below. Wontum listened. He also heard a movement within Manonie's apartment, and had hardly time to conceal himself behind the rubbish in the end of the hall, when she made her appearance. Tripping lightly toward the top of the stairs, she exclaimed, as if speaking her thoughts:

"Oh! perhaps he has come." She bent over the railing and listened. While thus engaged, the savage passed unseen into her room. He secreted himself readily behind the heavy curtains which draped the window, and awaited her return.

While she remained absent the savage had an opportunity of surveying her apartment. It would have been considered a luxurious one, even amid the surroundings of fashion. Upon a couch was reposing the child, little Harry Marshall. This was the son of her he once had loved, with a kind of barbarian passion. The son! It was the instrument of his designs upon father and mother! Again the fiend sat upon his lips, ready to scream its delight, but the monster forced the demon back to his heart to bide its time, when it should make the hills echo with its terrible joy.

He had not long to wait. The mother appeared. It was the first time Wontum had seen Manonie for three years; and it was not without some emotion on his part, something very seldom exhibited by the savage. As he gazed upon her his face grew as black as night, and he clutched his knife.

The mother approached the bed and bent over her child. It was sleeping calmly.

"It must have been my imagination," she exclaimed, "for my darling exhibits no further symptoms of pain. Oh, if I *should* lose him! But I am weary. Lieutenant Blair said that I must rest, or I should injure my health; so I must retire and sleep. It is strange. When I lived in the mountains I was never weary, and could keep the track, or drive my canoe night and day. But now that I have become accustomed to luxury, I tire so soon. Then my mind was free. Now, if my dear husband is absent from me only for an hour, I see before me images of death, and terror is ever present with me. If my child is restless, I magnify its danger. Yet I would not change for worlds, and be again what I was! Oh, no—it would be terrible—terrible. Don't let me think of losing what I have found! I wonder if my own parents loved me as I love my boy? I shall never see them, for they are dead. I never could survive his loss. Well, I will rest beside him." The mother knelt by the bedside. She raised her

clasped hands to heaven, and her lips moved, in humble, pen-
itential, thankful prayer.   Then she arose from her knees,
pressed her little one's hand gently to her lips, and laid herself by its side.   How the good angels must have fluttered
their pinions in pain, and longed to breathe into her ear the
words " fly—fly!"   Alas! the angels were in another world,
as far removed from the mother and child as life is removed
from death; and yet they were very near!

Overcome with watching, she slept.

The Evil One crept from his hiding-place and approached
the bed, clasping his knife, ready for immediate use, should it
be required.   Carefully he raised the child in his arms—so
carefully that he did not disturb the mother or the little sleeper.
Softly the Evil One opened the door and passed into the hall,
down the stairs and into the apartment of the murdered lieutenant.   Then he raised the window, and was surprised to
find that daylight was dawning.   The Evil One fears the light,
and so did Wontum.   The Evil One and himself were one,
that night.   In passing through it, the little fellow awoke, and,
beholding himself in the arms of such a monster, he set up
a wild cry.   It was echoed and reëchoed from the mother's
room.   Indeed, her shrieks were so frightful, that in a few
moments the entire garrison was aroused.

The Pawnee heard the cries of the mother, who had been
awakened by the screams of her child.   No time was to be
lost.   He therefore dashed boldly forward across the open
space toward the outer wall.   So unexpected was such an
event, and the guard so unprepared, that, before the pursuit
had fairly been commenced, the Indian actually had mounted
the outer wall.   A dozen muskets were leveled, but no one
dared fire, lest they should injure the child.

Leaping from the wall, the red monster ran like a deer toward the Laramie river.   Into its waters he plunged, and made
rapidly for the opposite shore.   The poor mother had thrown
up her window just in time to see her darling disappear.   For
a moment her strength failed, and she was helpless; but it was
a brief moment.   In a second of time she threw off her weak-
ness and put on her strength—strength to do and dare all
things.   The Woman became the Spirit Invincible.

Her cries were stilled and her sobs were smothered. A flame gleamed in her eyes almost supernatural. It was not the fire of madness, but the great light of love and devotion which burns upon every true mother's altar. With a bound she sprung through the window. It was a fearful plunge, but she appeared not in the least injured. With her hair streaming in the breeze, she darted for the spot where she had last seen her boy. Those who feared for her own life, and knowing that her own efforts could avail nothing, attempted to interrupt her, but in vain. She almost flew over the turf of the parade, and quickly reached the wall, dashed over it, and on into the river—on into the belt of timber beyond—disappearing like a meteor, in the gloomy depths of the jungle.

A brief examination resulted in finding the murdered lieutenant; but how it had all been done, no one could conjecture. A strong force at once left the fort in hot pursuit. This was unfortunate. They were attacked, and the slaughter became terrible. The savages were victorious, and Laramie, for the first time, fell into their hands. It soon became a mass of smoking ruins, and none lived to tell the tale of its fall, save those who had been fortunate enough to escape, early in the contest, to the adjoining mountains.

CHAPTER IV

A MOUNTAIN ADVENTURE—QUINDARO.

It was not an easy matter for Lieutenant Marshall and his new-found friends to make their way among the rocks, trees and thick undergrowth which it became necessary to encounter as they journeyed along the mountain ridges. Marshall became impatient, and, had it not been for the restraint of his companions, he would have taken the valley, regardless of the danger he might have there encountered.

Night came on and they paused for rest. And much they needed it; for the way was indeed a weary one. After the evening meal of dried meats had been partaken of, the party

entered into a conversation with regard to the intentions of
the savages and the extent of the damage they would be likely
to do before a sufficient force of the United States troops could
be brought against, to crush them. Oakley was of opinion
that the affair would end in smoke, while the hermit shook
his head dubiously. Of course, Marshall had all confidence
in the soldiery, but, he acknowledged, his present anxiety was
very great. A foreboding of disaster haunted and depressed
him in a distressing manner.

"If we could only jest lay our paws on that catamount as
calls himself the leader, we'd either make him stop the row,
or we'd fix his flint for him, by the stockin's!"

"What do you mean by that term?" asked Marshall of Oakley

"What?   Fixin' his flint?"

"Yes."

"Why, polishin' the critter off—makin' him hump! Givin'
him ' old hundred,' oney makin' the tune partikler meter, with
lots of bars and staves chucked in to fill up kinder."

"Well, I think I understand you. But, to whom do you
refer as the ' catamount?' "

"Wal, I reck'n it's Nemona, the Pawnee chief."

"I think," added the hermit, "that Wontum has really more
influence with the tribe than the chief himself. Nemona appears like a civilly disposed person; but the other is bloodthirsty and relentless."

"That's just as true as gospel preachin'. I tell you if
'twan't fur just one chap what lives down in that are valley,
you'd a' seen that red-skinned varmint hoein' a swath clean
through them few cabins as you see sprinkled around. But
even Wontum is fraiderer of *him* than all the sarpints on Rattlesnake Ridge."

"To whom do you refer?" asked Marshall.

"Wal, cap'n, that's a tough question to answer. The
amount of it is, nobody round these diggin's, unless it's my
gal Molly, knows any thing about him. And if *she* does, she
won't tell. Queer critters these gals is, to be sure."

"What do *you* call him?" asked Marshall, his interest visibly excited.

"Wal, it's some outlandish name as almost breaks my jaw
whenever I speak it. Molly calls him Quindaro."

"How happens it that your daughter is acquainted with the stranger and not yourself?'" asked John.

"Wal, ye see, John, I'm not much given to interferin' in the women folkses' matters; an' as Molly is a dootiful gal, I didn't press the subject. 'Cos I sed to myself: 'Jack, may hap they be loveyers,' an' when I was a-courtin' the old woman, I didn't want nobody else to come rootin' around—not a bit of it. Ef I war' goin' to court, I wa'r, an' didn't intend that anybody should interfere in *that* operation."

"How do you know that the intentions of this strange man are honorable toward your child?"

"Father John," exclaimed Oakley, as he started to his feet, "I'm down right surprised to hear you ask *such* a question. How do I know he means well towards my gal? I'll tell you how by askin' you a few questions. Don't you remember one dark night, about six years ago—Molly was a *little* gal then—that the reds came upon us an' began their cuttin's up; an' when I interfered, as I was in duty bound to do, and the knife of a savage was just at my throat, an' I thought it was all day with old Jack Oakley, that this man rushed in, an' catchin' the red by the neck, he pitched him clean through the winder? An' that warn't all. He went in like as he was goin' 'bout a week's work. Lord, but 'twas a purty sight! I warn't no whare, and I do consider myself some on a bear-hug. An' when he got through, and the reds had all taken to their heels like mad, he just took Molly up in his arms, kissed her just once, called her his darling, and then vanished like a streak, without waitin' to tell us who he was, or givin' me a chance to thank him."

"I remember you having informed me of this before," replied John.

"Wal, an' that wasn't the first time by a jug full, nor the last one either, that he has saved the settlers on the plains from the varmints. It appears as if he was always around when there is danger."

"I have heard of this Quindaro," said Marshall, "and, from what I can learn of his character, I do not think he is the person to deceive an innocent girl."

"Not by a long sight, cap'n. I tell you what it is, I *trust* my gal. An' I think that's the way to do. Why, sir, when

I lived down to St. Jo, we used to have lots of nabers. Me an' the old woman was just spliced then. Ye see, I alers said I'd marry a gal as I would love, and if I found that, I could *trust* her. I thought that was about as good an' evidence as I could have that I *loved* her. But I alers said that I wasn't goin' to court very long before gettin' spliced, an' I should kinder watch an' see what the gal's father and mother thought of her, an' take my 'pinion somethin' from that. So, when I went to see a gal, if I found that the old woman was watchin' an' listenin' an' bobbin' in and out the room every few seconds, or sendin' the little boy in, or all such tricks, I used to say to myself: ' Jack, that's enough for you. The mother *knows* the gal better than you do, and if *she* can't trust her, why should *you?*' An' when I *did* get married, an' had a daughter, I just said to myself: ' now, Jack, look out that you don't *insult* your little gal by onjust suspicions; 'cos if you *do*, you needn't be surprised if other folks insult her too.' No, sir; while I have confidence in my own child, I never expect to tell strangers, by my actions, that I have not. An' I know Molly *is* a good gal. I kinder reckon she don't know any thing about Quindaro, more than he's a kind o' hunter. But, if she does, an' don't tell her parents, it's because it's *his* secret, an' it will all come out right some day."

" You are right, Mr. Oakley," replied Marshall. " I honor your judgment."

" Call me Jack, if you please. Nobody hereabout knows *Mister* Oakley—not even my old woman."

" Well, Jack, you are right in the course you pursue. It is my opinion that Quindaro has some sufficient reason for his singular reserve ; and that he would not be likely to inflict wrong or bring disgrace upon others, I can well conceive. He has, I believe, a special spite against the savages."

" I hardly think that spite is the term which should be used in connection with him. He has never been known to molest a single Indian, or even a party, if they were *peaceable*. It is only when they are bent upon mischief that he makes his appearance ; and sometimes in an unaccountable manner."

" Have *you* ever seen him ?" asked Marshall of old John.

" I think I met him on one occasion," replied the hermit.

" Describe his appearance, if you please."

" I am not sure that I can do so. Oakley can do it, as he has met him more frequently."

" Never clap'd my eyes upon him more than half-a-dozen times. But I've measured him about the same as I measure a prairie-hen upon the wing."

" Well."

" Wal, he's about as tall as they get up men about these parts, an' he ain't no bean-pole either. He wears his hair about as long as Father John's ; but it is as black as it can be —black, sir, as a raven's breast, and as flowing as water."

" Then he is a *young* man ?" asked Marshall.

" I should think he was about thirty. But the most remarkable feature about him is his eyes. Why, sir, the reds are almost as afraid of them as they are of his rifle."

" What is there peculiar about them ?"

" Peculiar ! Wal, accordin' to my way of thinkin', fire and brimstone ain't nowhere. Why, sir, that night when he was fightin' for us, I just looked into his eyes once, and hang me, if I didn't feel as if streaks of lightning were curling all around my body. But this was only when his dander was up ; for, after all was safe, and he held Molly in his arms, an' looked at wife an' me, them eyes, sir, filled up with water. An' though that water was a-bilin' an' bubblin' out, it had put out the fire, an' they looked as mild as a woman's."

" Then you know nothing of his history ?"

" Nothing, until he came to the plains."

" Where does he reside ?"

" That's another secret. Nobody knows. Somewhere in the mountains, I suppose. In some cave, mayhap. Shouldn't wonder if he was something like the birds, skippin' around an' roostin' just where night found him."

" This is all very interesting, and somewhat singular, I confess," said Marshall. " But it is time to make arrangements for the night. It always has been my custom, when encamping for the night, especially in this dangerous country, to throw out a picket-guard. But, as our numbers are small, we will be compelled to dispense with them. Do you think it advisable that we should relieve each other at guard during the night ?" he asked of the old man.

" It is proper that a constant watch should be kept. We

may not be disturbed, but it is well to be on the safe side. We are on dangerous ground, and extreme caution is highly necessary."

At this moment the lieutenant's horse raised his head snuffed the air, and acted in a singular manner.*

When Marshall observed this movement in Dahlgren, he became alert.

" There are strangers near us."

" Savages, think you ?" asked the old man.

" I am satisfied that it is some person or persons who could scarcely be termed friends. Still I may be mistaken. Certain it is that some one or some thing is near us."

The horse, however, became more quiet, and, at length quietly prostrated himself upon the ground.

Oakley did not appear altogether satisfied. He moved un easily up and down, while his eyes wandered in every direc tion. Still, he could distinguish nothing in the darkness.

The old man and Marshall wrapped themselves in their blankets, and, making the earth their bed, were, to all appear ances, soon fast asleep. They took care, however, to find a place partially sheltered, which would protect them from any secret shot, if a foe was lurking near.

But *did* they sleep ? Ah, who could tell the conflicting emotions that wrung the heart of each ! Marshall, with his

* It has been remarked by many, that the instinct of the horse, especially when accustomed to a wild life, or to Indian and other warfare, is almost equal to that of the dog. That they are passive, and almost indifferent, in battle, is, in most cases, also true. They are often engaged, during the hot test of an artillery fire, in nibbling the grass, giving apparently no heed to the bursting shell. Indeed, instances have been known where horses have been wounded, and even their riders have not been aware of the fact until the poor beast had fallen to the earth.

An instance of this kind occurred at Gettysburg. A horse, attached to one of the batteries, was wounded, by a minie ball, in the shoulder. The ball passed a distance of not less than two feet under the skin before it force was spent. It did at last bury itself into the flesh, and made a bad wound. During the time the battery was engaged, the horse had stood perfectly quiet. Not even a start of fright or pain had been observed in the beast by his driver, who was standing constantly by his side.

At length, the battery was drawn off, and, for several hours, was not under fire, or in any position where it would have been possible for man or animal to have received a shot. It was not until a long time after the action that the wound was observed, and the course of the ball traced And yet, this very horse is said, on more than one occasion, to have "pricked up his ears and snuffed the air," as if conscious of approaching danger, *long before* the enemy had opened fire. This instinct appears most prominent in those animals which are accustomed to the secret mode of warfare of the savage or the guerrilla. Then their senses seem doubly acute, as many well-attested cases demonstrate.

present hopes and fears, thoughts of wife and ehild. The old man and the eonnecting link between the present and the past, which had left its furrows on his eheeks, and its sorrows in his silver locks.

Oakley was on guard. He kept himself "eovered" by a large tree, and sometimes listened with breathless silence. Once or twice he heard the rustling of the leaves and the breaking of a twig, whieh, to the experieneed hunter, always are evidences that to others might be deemed too trivial for attention.

It was near midnight. Marshall had twiee requested Oakley to let him take his plaee on guard, but the latter positively refused. The old man appeared to sleep soundly, although he held the long rifle, which he had brought with him, in a firm grasp.

Upon a sudden, the horse sprung up, and, throwing baek his ears, leaped forward with open mouth, making a furious attack upon some objeet eoneealed among the shrubbery. The yelping of a dog followed, whieh, judging by the sound, started from the spot. The horse then quietly returned.

Marshall and the old man had started to their feet.

"What think you of that?" asked Old John.

"Think? By hokey, there ain't but one thing to think about it."

"And what is that?"

"Wal, eap'n, that your hoss missed his aim, and got hold of the dog, instead of the Ingen."

"I know it. Keep close—*squat.*" Oakley threw himself upon the ground.

It was well for the others that they followed his example; for a stream of fire was seen, and the report of a rifle followed, close at hand.

Marshall was about to rush forward to the spot where his horse was standing, but the old man restrained him, saying :

"They won't toueh Dahlgren—they want him for their own use. We must keep elose and wateh the ehances. There are a number of the savages there, or they never would have ventured to fire that shot. It is likely they do not know our numbers. Daylight will develop something. In the mean time we must remain as much as possible under eover."

The night passed slowly away. There had been one or two attempts on the part of some one to get possession of the horse, but the animal defended himself in a most remarkable manner. There were, also, occasional noises, such as low whisperings, the moving of underbrush, and a low growl. But our friends kept close, preferring to await daylight, rather than the uncertainty of an action in the dark.

The day came at length, but not a living being was visible.

"Come," said Marshall, "let us continue our journey."

"No," replied the old man. "There is work before us yet. The savages are concealed behind those rocks, and the moment we show ourselves, it will be to meet death."

"What is to be done?" asked Marshall.

"We must outwit them. Oakley, you and Marshall remain here, while I take a scout around and see what is going on. Oh! you need not look surprised. I am not so old but that I am yet able to climb the rocks, or that I am entirely unacquainted with savage warfare."

The old man seized his rifle, and started down the mountain side. An hour passed, and there was a movement among the rocks, and the plumed heads of several savages appeared. Then one of them ventured forth. Marshall drew his revolver and fired. This was a very injudicious action, for several of the Indians, judging by the single shot that there could not be many opposed to them, rushed forth. The lieutenant discharged the other five barrels, but without further effect than the wounding of three of the Indians. Four others remained untouched, and these came bounding forward. They well knew that the shots fired were not by the hands of hunters, whom they feared more than the regular soldiers.

Oakley raised his true rifle, and the foremost Indian fell with a wild yell. Three now remained, and their pieces were loaded. It was therefore the policy of Oakley to prevent the savages from using them if possible, and to depend upon the close struggle and the knife.

But, before the encounter commenced, a wild yell arose but a few yards from the savages, and then a shot. Another of their number fell. The two remaining turned to encounter their unexpected foe, but, the heavy barrel of a rifle came crashing down upon the head of another, and he rolled upon the earth. The rescuer seized the last remaining savage, and, as if he had been a mere child in size, hurled him down among the broken rocks, with such force, that scarcely a groan followed his fall.

"QUINDARO!" cried Oakley, as he recognized the strange man.

"Quindaro, at your service!"

And without waiting for another word, the new-comer started rapidly up the rugged mountain again.

"Stay, Quindaro, stay," called Oakley and Marshall.

"No! I have more work before me. We shall meet again."

It was not long before the old hermit returned, and the party continued their journey. Arriving at Laramie river, they found no difficulty in procuring a small boat, and, as they had only to float with the stream, before nightfall Marshall and Old John reached the fort, or rather its ruins. Oakley, having volunteered to see the horse Dahlgren safely down, followed the stream at his leisure, and crossed at the fort before darkness set in.

The savages had left the vicinity of the fort, and a few of the soldiers had returned. Of these Marshall could glean but a confused account of what had happened. Of his wife and child they knew nothing.

What agony filled the soul of the husband and father! Uncertainty with regard to their fate appeared really worse than the positive knowledge of their death. And the image of the Pawnee miscreant rose up before him in all its horror. He sunk upon the ground and groaned in very agony of soul. Old John touched him gently and spoke:

"Come, don't yield to such feelings. You must *act* now. No doubt she is still alive. It must be *our* work to rescue her or to perish for her sake."

At this moment a soldier came up, who gave a detail of the events, and indicated the direction taken by Wontum and the child, followed by the mother. Marshall was about to start in immediate pursuit, but the body of soldiers which had been sent after the murdered party, having just arrived, he was detained until the morning following.

Oakley and the old man took their departure, however—not waiting for the soldiery. They proposed to work in their own way.

2

CHAPTER V.

THE ENCOUNTER.

WONTUM did not expect that the mother would follow him so closely. He had calculated upon drawing a number of the soldiers out of the fort, and, if this could be done, a successful attack might be made upon them. This resulted as he anticipated. He had no doubt the fort would fall, but, in case of failure, as he could not secure both his victims at that time, he hoped that the mother would eventually seek him in the mountains in order to regain possession of her boy.

A gleam of savage joy lit up his face, as he saw Manonie spring from the wall and follow toward the river, having no doubt but that she would continue her pursuit. He knew that three years had not altogether eradicated the habits she had acquired while living with the Indians, and that river or mountain would not be a barrier to the chase.

And so it proved; for the frantic mother paused not when she reached the river, but, plunging in, she swam for the opposite shore, with her old skill.

Wontum had seated himself, and was watching the progress of the fight which was going on in and near the fort. Seeing that he was not pursued by the troops, he determined to await the result of the encounter. Manonie would reach him in a few moments, but this was as he wished.

The struggle was a brief one, and Laramie had fallen.

Manonie now approached the savage. Little Harry was seated upon the earth by the side of the Indian, sobbing, but when he saw his mother, he started up and sprung into her arms. She then turned as if to retrace her steps, but Wontum caught her, saying:

"Wild Bird, sit."

"Not by you, monster that you are!" she cried.

"Wontum no monster. Wontum great warrior. He kill enemy."

"And *steal* little children. Wontum is a mean thief."

"Ugh!"

"Why have you thus taken my child? Is it not mean business for a great warrior?"

"Don't Wild Bird want her child?"

"Oh! yes. Give him to me and I will always be your friend."

"Be wife?"

"How can I be your wife, when I am already married?"

"Ugh! Wild Bird must go with Wontum."

"Where?"

"To wigwam in Pawnee country. Wild Bird *shall* be his squaw, or he kill boy. Come."

The savage seized the child and started on his return toward the fort. He had seen the result of the fight. This time he procured a small canoe, and, entering it, he soon landed near the scene of carnage. Manonie had remained close by his side.

After the destruction of the fort, or its interior buildings, the savages appeared to be satisfied. At the command of Wontum, they commenced their retreat. Among the captures made were a number of fine horses. Manonie was placed upon one of these, while Wontum mounted another, taking the child in his arms. He started off, bidding the mother follow him, which she did without hesitancy.

The object of the Indian now appeared to be gained, or, at least, the principal part of it. The Wild Bird and her child were in his power. The father's heart would be wrung, even if he was not captured or slain. It was not the savage's purpose to fight again, if it could be avoided. He knew, by what he had overheard at the fort, that a body of men had gone up the valley. On their return, it was likely they would come down the Platte river road; hence, the chief gave orders to fall back by the way of Laramie Peak. It was quite likely the soldiers would follow when they learned what had occurred. It was the chief's intention, therefore, to reach Devil's Gate, where the whites' artillery could not be brought to bear against them, as the savages entertained a mortal horror of those two little field-pieces which they had once faced at South Pass.

Manonie, knowing it would be useless to plead with the

savage, was silent. She was a prisoner, it was true; yet she could not believe that Wontum would injure her or the boy; and, might she not, by some stratagem, effect her escape? Her chief cause for anguish was the unaccountable absence of her husband, and her uncertainty as to his fate.

They had reached the base of the peak, when Wontum suddenly halted, making a sign. to his warriors to do the same. Then they moved rapidly into a thick covering of mountain willow which grew upon the bank of a little creek, which would effectually conceal them from any party passing the main road.

They were scarcely concealed when Manonie heard the clatter of horses' feet, and, judging by the sound, a large party was approaching. It must be her friends: would not her rescue be now effected? Perhaps her husband was one of the number! She now saw that the savages did not intend an attack, as they prostrated themselves upon the ground. It would be necessary for her to give the alarm, which she determined to do, although there would be great danger to herself and child in the fight sure to ensue.

But in this she was doomed to disappointment; for, just as the advance of the approaching horsemen had arrived nearly opposite the spot where she was concealed, Wontum placed the point of his knife at the breast of the boy, and said:

"If Wild Bird make noise, me kill."

Manonie shuddered and remained silent. The clatter of hoofs, the jingle of swords against the riders' spurs, the voices of men and the laughter of others, fell upon her ears, but she dared not speak. Friends were near, yet unconscious of her presence, and would soon leave her far behind, still a wretched prisoner. A single scream would call their attention, and yet it would be the death of her boy. The last horsemen were passing. Hope did not sink within her. Her time had not yet come.

Just at that moment the horse upon which Wontum was seated, began pawing the earth. This act was followed by a whinny, also repeated by the horse on which Manonie rode. The horsemen came to a halt. A large dog, too, ran into the willow shrubbery, and then back to his masters, setting up a fearful howling.

Ugh! Bad — much bad," exclaimed Wontum. He glanced around him, and then, without uttering a word, dismounted, and ran swiftly up the side of the peak, still holding the boy in his arms. The mother followed, evidently determined not to lose sight of her precious treasure.

Nor was this movement made an instant too soon; for the report of a cannon was heard, and the canister came tearing through the shrubbery. The horse upon which Manonic had been seated, reared, and then, with a cry almost human in its tones, plunged forward, and fell to the earth, dead.

The savages sprung up with a wild and defiant yell, and rushed from their concealment. But they were met by a galling fire, and nearly a third of their number bit the dust.

The horsemen consisted of over one hundred United States dragoons, well mounted and armed, each man carrying a carbine slung at his side, and a brace of pistols. Hearing the whinny of the horse, they at once divined the true state of the case. Immediately forming in line, they brought their artillery, which consisted of two light six-pound field-pieces, into position. Of course, they were not aware of the presence of captives, but had no doubt of its being an Indian ambush. The dog—a sagacious animal—on several occasions had been the means of detecting the concealed foe. Therefore, the guns were charged, and the iron hail hurled into the willow, as the best method of bringing out the human tigers concealed there.

The troops were surprised to see so large a number, but were prepared to receive them. A second and a third volley was poured in upon them, but, as these were from the pistols, they were less effective than the first, which was given with the carbine. The cannon, however, cut them down terribly. It was heaven's thunder to them, from which there was no escape.

Then came a charge, and a hand-to-hand encounter. The savages fought with a desperation seldom equaled, but they could not long stand before the ponderous death-strokes of the horsemen's sabers. Besides, they were without a leader. The voice of Wontum, which had cheered them on in many a fight, was not heard. Many had not seen his movement, and supposed he had fallen with the others.

Although the battle raged fiercely, it was brief. In half an hour after the savages were discovered, two-thirds of their number were either killed or wounded, and the others, panic-stricken, were flying up the ragged side of Laramie Peak.

Wontum had not been seen by any of the soldiers, as his flight was covered by the thick wood. He advanced to a safe distance, and then stopped to watch the progress of the battle. He was not altogether confident of victory, but did not anticipate so decided a defeat. When he saw the result, it was to rave like a madman. He had not left his warriors from any personal fear; but revenge still was the passion uppermost in his soul, to secure which he must retain possession of Manonie. He still held the child, and the poor mother preferred any fate to leaving it.

It was impossible for the cavalry to pursue the fugitives up the rocky steep, and they at once turned their attention to their dead and wounded. In killed there were but four, but there were over fifty wounded. The Indians had fought principally with the tomahawk and knife.

Manonie was doomed to witness the departure of her friends, and her heart almost sunk within her. They were not even aware that she was a captive, or, surely, they would make further efforts for her rescue. She endeavored to draw from the savage his intentions, but he was silent and sullen. She inquired about her husband, but a bitter frown was the only answer.

The journey was now renewed. It was a weary one, as they were now without horses. They did not follow the valley, but kept along the mountain ridge. It was nearly dark when the party, who had joined Wontum after their defeat, halted at the foot of a ridge, upon the bank of a beautiful stream of water. There was no sign of a road or trail near, and Manonie could not tell any thing with regard to her location, although she was, or had been, quite familiar with the plains and mountains. She was satisfied, however, that the stream was one of the little tributaries of the Platte, and began making her calculations for escape during the night.

The camp was formed. Manonie was placed in the center of a circle made by living savages, and little Harry by her side. But, before he slept, Wontum stripped the bark from some young saplings, and, making a strong thong, tied it firmly around her body, and then to his own. This seemed, indeed, to seal her fate, for what escape could there be from that thong?

It was not long before the heavy breathing of the band convinced Manonie that most of them were sleeping. It had been a day of fatigue for them, as well as for herself. Her child had fallen asleep in her arms, and it was with difficulty she could keep her own eyes from closing. But she had resolved upon a desperate attempt to escape, despite her bands and critical position.

With this intention, her first action was to release herself from the thong which bound her. This she accomplished by gnawing it with her teeth. She was about to move from the spot, when Wontum caught her by the wrist, and held it with a grasp so firm, that it caused her to utter an exclamation of pain. This was, apparently, unnoticed by the savage, and Manonie became convinced that it was only a movement of chance, and that he still was sleeping. He had probably set his mind so much upon the subject of preventing her escape, that even in his sleep any movement upon her part would disturb him. She raised herself partially and listened. The Indian was breathing hard and regular; but, occasionally, he gave vent to ejaculations of rage, although the words were undistinguishable. He was implacable even in his dreams— a savage, even in his slumbers.

Manonie gazed around her. Every thing denoted profound sleep. It was the time for action. The hot blood mounted to the temples of the poor girl as her eyes fell upon the knife of the chief. It was in his belt, and glittered in the dim moonlight ominously. She cautiously reached forth her hand and drew the weapon from the belt, to gaze upon its keen point, still red with the blood of poor Blair. A shudder passed over her frame. Then she gazed into the face of her child, who was sweetly sleeping; then down the little stream, and then up into the clear blue sky, with its millions of stars; then again upon the face of the monster whose fiendish nature had brought her into her present situation, and wrought such misery. Was it right for her to strike the blow which would free the world from such a wretch? This appeared to be the only course. But would her hand be firm, and her aim true? And would heaven smile on such an act?

The poor girl raised her eyes to heaven, and, in the faith of a true believer, implored its aid.

" Oh, thou Great Spirit, help me to do the right!"

It was a brief but earnest prayer, which seemed to give her strength and courage. She raised the knife, and would have buried it to the hilt in his bosom, but, at that instant, the grasp which the savage had fastened upon her left wrist was loosened, and she was free! The knife was lowered, and the monster was spared.

Cautiously she raised herself, and took the child in her arms. She gazed searchingly around. All was quiet. It was a moment of terrible anxiety. Carefully she stepped over the sleepers. She could hear the beatings of her own heart.

In a moment she stood beside the water, free. And yet, *not* free. For, at that most critical moment, little Harry awoke, and cried with fear. This aroused Wontum. He sprung after the captives. The poor mother saw him as he sprung to his feet. She knew that escape would be impossible, and, with the most remarkable presence of mind, she said, loud enough to be heard by the savage:

" Does little Harry want a drink of water? He shall have it. Manonie will give it to him."

Taking her little cup, she dipped it in the stream, and held it up for the child, who drank heartily. Then the mother added:

" Now, Harry, go to sleep again, that's a good child."

" Where is papa?" asked the boy. The question was like an arrow in the breast of the mother, but she replied:

" Never mind, darling, we will see papa soon."

" To-morrow?"

" Perhaps to-morrow."

" Where is that bad man that took me away from my home?"

" Hush!"

" Here!" exclaimed the savage, as he approached the spot. " Here bad man."

Wontum led the captive back to the center of the circle. She gave up all further hope of escape that night, and resigned herself to sleep. In the stillness, a voice came over the valley, low, but distinct:

"*You should have struck the blow!*"

Wontum heard the voice, and started up—so indistinctly, however, that he was not sure whether it really was a voice, or his own fancy. But it brought consolation to Manonie. True, she did not recognize the tones as familiar, but it *must* be a friend. She was not, indeed, deserted, and was content.

The night passed slowly away; and the mother and child, overcome by the toils of the previous day, slept, thus gaining fresh strength for coming trials.

CHAPTER VI.

FRIENDS.

OLD JOHN and Oakley, after leaving the fort, or rather its ruins, seated themselves upon the bank of the Laramie, and entered into a conversation with regard to the events which had occurred, and the course it was best for them to pursue. Oakley often had met Manonie while she was yet residing with the savages, and was, like all others, fondly attached to her. But Old John never had seen her, which was somewhat singular, as he had been in the vicinity even some years previous to her marriage with Lieutenant Marshall. What was still more strange, he had never heard of her, until he met her husband at his cabin on the mountain side. He evidently was more of a *solitaire* than he thought.

It was at length decided that they should follow up the trail of the savages, and when Wontum was found, one of them should keep a close watch upon his movements, and ascertain in what manner the captives were to be disposed of, while the other should return and report to the garrison. A thorough examination convinced them that the savage must have accompanied the main party, as there were no signs of a separate trail.

Their stay had been so short at the fort, that they had not learned of the second encounter between the troops and the savages. With early dawn they set out, and pursued the trail, but were somewhat puzzled by the tracks of the incoming horsemen which had almost obliterated those of the savages. They were of the opinion that the latter had turned aside on the approach of the soldiers, and that no encounter had taken place.

A few hours' rapid walk brought them to the battle-ground. A search revealed the fact that the Indians had concealed themselves. The horse which had been taken from the fort, and was killed by the cannon's discharge, was still upon the spot.

The professional hunter is as shrewd in following the trail as the Indian himself, and oftentimes more so. He can detect the slightest evidence, such as the bending of a bush, a broken twig, or the disturbance of a leaf. And thus Oakley traced the course taken by the savage and Manonie, the former by the huge proportions of his moccasin, and the captive by the tiny footprint. The evidence was plain where they had seated themselves upon the ground, and then the new direction taken by them along the "Black Hills" ridge, toward Deer Creek.

It was decided, after they were perfectly satisfied upon this point, that one of them must return immediately to the fort, and inform Marshall of these particulars. But *which* it should be was not a question so easily settled, *both* claiming the right to encounter the danger, and to *enjoy* the excitement of following the trail.

"Wal, now, John," said Oakley, "you're grit an' no mistake. But, Lord love you, I don't b'lieve you know any more 'bout Injuns then a baby. Why, you're so pious-like that you wouldn't hurt a muskeeter any way, an' I don't think that, in your old days, you is agoing to l'arn new tricks."

"Perhaps I am not so ignorant with regard to their habits as you may imagine. I think I could follow a trail, or even strike down a savage, if justice required me to do so."

"No! Could ye now? Wal, perhaps ye might. But I don't see how you *can* know any thing about their habits, for you're alers up at your cab'n in the mountain, readin' your books an' sich like ; but I tell you what it is, John : you may have a power of knowledge so far as book eddication goes, but I cac'late them kind of books dou't tell much 'bout Injuns. You've got to study the great book as lays spread out before ye here." Oakley pointed to the surrounding scenery, and the old man bowed his head with reverence. In a moment he said :

" Well, Oakley, let us give our opinions as to the intentions of the savage abductor, and his purpose in carrying off the child."

" All right. Go ahead. Give us yer idees, an' we'll see how much yer kin read ther savage."

" He will follow the Black Hills till he reaches Deer creek."

" I think so, percisely. Go ahead ag'in."

" And then push directly across the valley, until he reaches the Sweetwater."

" Jest my 'pinion ag'in."

" And will not pause until he has reached Devil's Gate."

" Jes' so," my old friend. " Try yer tongue ag'in."

" There he will consider himself safe, and will be so, comparatively ; for it will be impossible to bring artillery to bear upon the savages when concealed iu the caves, and a few hundred of them might successfully hold at bay a large army."

" Jes' so, sir. Right ag'in. But, I rather reck'n there'd be another way to get at 'em."

" I understand you. They must be surrounded and starved out. This will be the only course if they succeed in reaching the Gate."

" If they succeed in reachin' it ? An' how in thunder do ye cac'late to prevent 'em from doin' so, will yer please ter demonstrate ?"

" Well, I will demonstrate : How many of the war-party do you suppose there are ?"

" Wal, I think I can tell pretty sartin. They didn't expect to be followed, an' so they don't go single-file an' tread in each other's tracks. Let me see." Oakley examined around for several minutes, and at length replied :

" I reck'n there's about sixty on ' em. And now what's yer plan ?"

"It is to have the Indians intercepted before they reach the Sweetwater."

"Wal, s'pose we should intercept 'em; what are we to do agin' sixty on 'em?"

"You don't understand me. You are to make all possible haste back to the fort. Inform Marshall. The troops are mounted, and the savages are not. It will not be difficult to reach the river before they do."

"Yes. That's all very nice. But, why do you say that *I* am to go back?"

"You prefer that *I* should go?"

"Yes, John. I don't think you are as good at scoutin' as I be; besides, you are too old to be knockin' around the woods after Injuns. If you go to the fort, you will have a chance to ride."

"Why, Oakley, you are almost as old as myself."

"Wal, that's so; but then, ye see, I have been used to roughin' on it until I'm as tough as an oak knot, an' twice as strong as you, ef you be bigger."

"Do you think so?"

"I do jest think so. If you think you can handle old Jack Oakley, come right along an' try it. You'll find I'm some on a b'ar-hug."

The old man smiled, and, advancing, seized Oakley. Jack made three or four desperate efforts to lift the old man from his feet, but could not do it. During the time, John stood quietly, although his grasp was firm. At length, by a sudden movement, he caught Jack in a manner termed by the boys a "hip-lock," and, making an effort at the same moment, hurled him entirely over his head. Oakley came down on the ground like a huge log. But he sprung to his feet with a "whoop," and seized the hermit a second time; but, quick as thought, he was again hurled high into the air, and came down with a tremendous "chug."

This time Jack raised himself slowly to his feet, rubbed his arms, neck and head, looked at the old man, who stood smiling before him, with a peculiar gaze, not unmingled with admiration, and then exclaimed:

"Je-ru-sha! but you *are* some. Guv us yer hand."

"You think I would make a good Indian fighter?" Old John smilingly asked.

"Fust chop. An' I'll tell you what it is. You must go at it. 'Tis a shame for you to be tucked up in that cabin of yours, when ye ought to be in the mountains killin' half a dozen reds in a day."

"I could not take the life of a savage, even, unless I was justified in doing so in my own defense, or for the safety of others."

"But, we are at war now, and every red we meet is our enemy."

"So I shall look upon every one, if he gives the slightest evidence of a hostile purpose, and I shall act accordingly. But, now tell me, who is to return to the fort?"

"Wal, I cac'late I'll have to be the chap. An' no time is to be lost; so hoora for father John, once the old hermit, but now a reg'lar Injun fighter, an' one as can flop old Jack Oakley, as easy as the old woman can flop a hoe-cake." Saying which, he commenced his return to the fort.

Oakley soon reached the foot of the mountains, and struck off across the valley. As he rubbed his shoulders, he exclaimed:

"By the great jewallopers, but that old feller is a snorter, an' no mistake. I wonder where he l'arned that hug?"

"To whom do you refer?" asked a voice near him.

Oakley started. There, not two rods away, he saw the speaker, seated upon the bank of a small stream.

"Quindaro!"

"Yes. What are you doing here, Oakley?"

"Oh! the old boy is to pay ginerally." Oakley then went on to explain all the particulars of the events which had recently occurred, so far as they were known to him.

"And where is Mary?" asked Quindaro.

'Who?"

'Your daughter."

'Oh, yes. Molly. That's what ɪ call the gal, although I believe the old woman *did* say that she was rightly named Mary."

"Where is she?"

"Safe up at the old hermit's cabin—she an' the old woman, too."

"Do you really think she will be safe there?"

"Oh, bless ye, yes. Thar' ain't a red this side of California as would touch Old John. But I'll tell ye a secret ef ye will keep it to yerself."

"What is it?"

"That old man is death on a b'ar-hug. I found that out a few moments ago." And old Jack rubbed his shoulders again.

"Where is the old man?" asked Quindaro, with a sudden interest.

"He was up there not fifteen minutes ago, but, he's started off on the trail, an' I shouldn't be a bit surprised if he did some tall work. I'll tell ye another secret. The old man is goin' to join us agin' the reds. That's true as gospel preachin'; 'cos he said so, an' he ain't the one to lie about any thing. But, why hain't ye been up to see Molly in so long a time? She's kinder takin' it to heart I reck'n, for the gal's grown pale an' the like, and she don't laugh an' sing as she used to do when we first settled in the plains."

"Oh, Mr. Oakley, these troubles are enough to drive the smile even from the face of nature itself, or cause the blue heavens to frown in anger. Why have I not been to visit you? It is because I have so much work to do here. And while the war lasts, I can devote myself to but one object. It is true, I wear the image of your daughter ever in my heart; but there is a wound there from which the blood flows so freely, that it hides from my view all but that which caused it. When I am amply avenged, then I will visit you—but not until then—no, not until then." The speaker was visibly affected.

"You must excuse me, Mr. Quindaro, but I see you're an eddicated man, an' I'm afeard my poor Molly won't be no match for you. But you won't—oh, I know I'm an old fool, an' ought to be kicked for askin' such a question—but I *do* love my gal so much that it would break my eld heart, tough as it is, if any thing should happen to her."

"Well, what were you going to ask?"

"You wouldn't win the love of my poor gal and then leave her to break her heart and die?"

Quindaro started to his feet, and gazed in silence upon Oakley.

"Oh, you needn't say that you won't, because I know it;

and you may kiek me if you like for askin' such a thing. It was only a passin' thought. I alers believed you were a first-chop, right honorable man, an' I think so yet. But you would excuse me if you knew what it was to be the father of a most dootiful an' devoted daughter."

The powerful frame of Quindaro trembled with emotion. He covered his face with his hands; but, at length, he raised his head, and answered:

"No, Mr. Oakley, I do not know what it is to be a father. But I *do* know what it is to be a son and a brother. And I know what it is to lose all. Oh, it was a dreadful night!" he continued, as if speaking his own thoughts rather than addressing another, " a night of horror! Oh! the streams of blood, the dying shrieks of those so dear, the crackling flame, and—but I *am* avenged, although not fully so!"

The heart of the strong man heaved in the intensity of his feelings, the hot blood mounted to his temples, while his eyes gleamed like living coals. Oakley gazed uuon him with some degree of surprise. He had felt sure that his cause of grief had some connection with the savages, but this was the first time a word had been spoken by which he could get the slightest clue as to the real facts.

"Did the Injuns do this?" he asked.

"Ay, the accursed Pawnees."

"Did they kill your folks?"

"Yes; father, mother, sister, brothers—all—all perished but myself."

"Are you *sure* all were killed?"

"Sure of it? Yes. I saw their mangled bodies stretched out before me."

"Did you see 'em buried fur sartin?"

"No. I barely escaped with my own life. But, when I returned, a few days after, I saw five new-made graves, and this was sufficient for me."

"And you followed the Pawnees?"

"Yes. I hovered around them while they lived near Willow Lake, and, when they came to the mountains, followed them. I have had life for life, years ago, but I will not bate one jot of my revenge or cease my work until the accursed race has been blotted from existence. Already my very name is a terror to them, but it shall become doubly so. I will pursue them to extermination—the monsters!"

"Where is your home, Quindaro?"

"Among the rocks in the mountains, in the valleys, by the river's side—anywhere, if duty calls me. Quindaro is like the wild bird, free to go where he pleases."

"Have you ever met old Father John?"

"I have seen him, I think, but have never met him face to face."

"Quindaro, promise me one thing."

"What is it?"

"That you will visit the old hermit soon as you get a chance."

"To what end?"

"No matter. Promise me."

"Well, I will do so. But I must now be off. I shall follow the trail of those savages. Perhaps I can succeed in rescuing this lady and her child, of whom you were speaking. And I may meet or overtake the old hermit, as you say he has gone in that directon." Quindaro extended his hand, shook that of old Jack warmly, then started off, at a rapid pace, up the Black Hill range.

Oakley gazed after him until he was lost to view, and then exclaimed:

"I'd be willin' to bet my scalp against the fust red-skin's I meet, that if he does overtake Old John he'll find his father in right-down earnest! They are as like as two peas! Somethin' tells me they are father and son. Whew!—what if it should be? But I must be off, for I'm losin' time."

Oakley now started for the fort, which he at length reached in safety. At once calling for Marshall, he detailed all the facts. It was a great consolation for the husband and father to learn that two such men as Old John and Quindaro were upon the trail of the savages.

Arrangements were quickly made for pursuit. A body of nearly two hundred soldiers had just arrived from Fort Jefferson, therefore a considerable number could be spared, and still leave a strong garrison behind.

Before daybreak of the third day after the massacre in the fort, all was in readiness, and Lieutenant Henry Marshall filed out of Laramie, at the head of two hundred and fifty horse-men and two pieces of artillery. Hope beat high in his heart as the cavalcade dashed up the valley toward the clear Sweetwater, which they hoped to be able to reach by the evening of the following day. Oakley rode in the advance, acting as guide.

CHAPTER VII.

THE MESSENGER.

THE morning dawned. It was beautiful and bright. The little streams, that danced and sparkled in the sunlight, vied with the fresh songsters in their music. It was a scene to inspire joy in the heart of man, or even soften the savage breast.

But the heart of Wontum knew no pity. He sat by the waters of the beautiful Deer creek, silent, his brow black as midnight, and his snake-like eyes fixed upon his victim. Poor Manonie shrunk from his gaze. She held her child close to her breast; this appeared to be her only joy. But she thought of the voice she had heard. "You should have struck the blow." She could not be mistaken, for the sound had aroused the savage, and even now he would cast his eyes suspiciously around, as if he half suspected the presence of some dreaded foe. Why was he hesitating? Did he fear to advance? Manonie could see beyond her a beautiful valley, which she at once recognized, and knew that it stretched far away to the Sweetwater, a distance of over fifty miles, only occasionally broken by sharp knolls and gentle-sloping rides. She hoped the savage would take his course through this valley, as he would be compelled to pass the cabins of many of the settlers. She did not even hope that they could be any present help to her, but she thought some white might see her, and thus be able to send some word to her husband, of her safety and of her whereabouts.

She arose to her feet, and strolled leisurely along the bank

of the stream. Little Harry had attempted to follow, but
Wontum detained him. The little fellow turned and struck
the savage a violent blow in the face. This, instead of making the chief angry, rather pleased him, for a half-smile played
around his repulsive mouth, and he muttered :

"Ugh !—good ! Make Injun-brave !"

He patted the boy upon the head, but the child had too
vivid a recollection of the occurrences of the previous day to
"make friends" with his enemy. He only showed his
"temper" the more.

Manonie kept on her way until she had reached a distance
of perhaps twenty rods from the savages. Her purpose was
not suspected by Wontum, although he watched her with an
eager and an eagle eye.

She cast searching glances around her, hoping to see the
person from whom the message proceeded the night before.
All at once, she was startled; something fell at her feet. It
was a pebble, to which was attached a bit of paper. She
grasped it as the reprieved man would clutch a document
which prolonged his life. She cast back a glance at the savage, to notice if her movements had been detected, but Wontum was still toying with the child. She tore the paper from
the stone to which it was attached, and read :

"Hope ! To-night you shall be free. Your husband is
aware of your situation and is making every effort for your
rescue. I am your friend and shall remain near you."

Manonie raised her eyes, and directly before her, not twenty
yards distant, peering over a fallen tree, she saw a pair of dark
eyes gazing earnestly upon her. The stranger raised himself
partially from concealment, placed his finger upon his lips,
indicating silence, and then disappeared from view.

Manonie could scarcely suppress the cry of wild delight
which trembled upon her lips, and the first impulse was to
bound forward into the arms of the stranger. But, with an
effort she controlled her emotion, and again turned toward the
place where her child and Wontum were seated. She trembled violently, and clasped little Harry to her breast in apparent rapture. To this, however, the Indian gave no heed.

She had not heard any word from the stranger, but that
look thrilled her. Nor did she recollect ever having seen him

beforc. But, he brought her hope, which amounted almost to certainty, as she could see the realization, but a short time distant, of her restoration to loved and loving hearts.

To-night. Oh! was she to be free to-night? Was she indeed to meet the idol of her soul again—be his forevermore? But, how was this to be accomplished? Was there to be another battle? If so, her husband might be killed. Around her were nearly seventy powerful savages, and she knew of but *one* friend near. Still, she felt a confidence in the dear, treasured message which had promised her freedom, even though there was a possibility of failure.

The savages now arose, and made preparations to continue their journey. With grief Manonie saw they intended to avoid the valley. They continued along the ridge of hills, but the plain below was visible most of the time, as the mountain was sparsely timbered. It was a weary journey for Manonie. On several occasions she was compelled to pause for rest. The advance of Wontum was much delayed in consequence. The savages appeared much annoyed at this, and gave vent to their feelings by angry looks and words, which Manonie readily understood, as she had not forgotten the language which she had learned in infancy.

On one occasion a dispute arose. One of the savages declared that Wontum was waging the war for his own selfish purposes, and that he had only commenced it for the sake of capturing the pale-face squaw, and this had cost them over a hundred warriors. And he appealed to those around him to put the girl to death, as her scalp was worth more than herself alive, and she never would become a squaw again, but would always prove a source of trouble. The boy should be saved, as he was now so young that he would soon forget his parents, and perhaps become a useful member of their tribe. He had given, even at his age, evidences of much spirit, and perhaps would become a great warrior.

Poor Manonie listened to this conversation with a painful interest. She gazed furtively around her, hoping to catch a glimpse of her strange friend, but he was as invisible as a spirit. It was finally decided that, as she *belonged* to their tribe, in spite of her marriage with the pale-face, they had no right to kill her without the sanction of the head chief. So she was to be taken before Nemona upon their arrival at Devil's Gate.

The sun was just sinking from sight when Wontum paused, and began the arrangements for their night camp. The circle was formed as before. In the center a few young saplings were drawn together at the top, and fastened. These were covered with brush and leaves, until quite a comfortable wigwam or covering had been formed. Manonie watched the proceedings with some degree of interest.

She was now seated upon a point where she could plainly descry a large portion of the valley. Oh! how eagerly she watched the distance, hoping to see the troops merge into the open space from the narrow ravine which skirts Horse-shoe creek! But she was doomed to disappointment: no troops appeared.

Wontum came to her side, and seated himself upon the ground. He gazed at her steadily for several moments. There was a peculiar expression upon his face. Manonie could not divine its meaning. At length he said, speaking half in the Pawnee tongue, and half in his broken English:

"You tried to kill me last night!"

Manonie started. She did not think for a moment that the savage was aware of her attempt upon his life. The knife had almost been in the act of descending, and yet he had not moved at the time. She had returned the weapon to his belt, and still he appeared to sleep. How he had discovered the fact, she could not tell; and yet, he had done so. The crimson which mounted to her face as she heard these words, was a tell-tale to the Indian, for he asked:

"Why you want to kill Wontum?"

Manonie, seeing that it was useless to deny the act, replied:

"I did not wish to kill you, unless it became necessary to do so in order to gain my liberty."

"Then you *did* try to kill Wontum?"

"Yes."

"Why not do it, den?"

"Because, at the moment I was about to strike the blow, you released my hand which you had been holding, and I thought I could escape without committing the deed. But, how did *you* know I made such an attempt?"

Wontum pointed to his knife, and said:

"You draw my knife. You no careful when you put it back in my belt. You put it in bullet-pouch! Why you wish to escape from me?"

"That I may return to my husband, of course."

"But Wontum shall never let child go." Manonie groaned. "And shall soon have husband *prisoner.* Him I burn! You be Wontum's squaw, den I no burn. Wontum want Wild Bird for squaw, and shall have her, or burn husband."

"Then he will die, for I shall never be your squaw. But my dear husband, he is not yet in your power, and I don't think ever will be. If you would save your own life, you had better set me free at once, for my husband's revenge will be sure and terrible."

"Ugh! Wontum no fear soldier pale-face! Soldier poor man in fight. Let him come. I shall be glad to meet him at Devil's Gate."

Manonie's quick and ever alert eye caught a glimpse of what she believed to be a human figure moving among the rocks at some distance from her. She was not positive, as the shadow appeared suddenly, and as quickly vanished. She averted her eyes from the spot, in order that the Indian's attention might not be attracted in that direction. A smile lit up her face. This Wontum observed and asked:

"Wild Bird thinks pleasant thoughts."

"I was thinking of my friends, and the revenge they shall visit upon you."

"Ugh! Wild Bird expect them to-night?" A significant smile rested upon the face of the savage, and she feared he knew more of the stranger than she had supposed. But this could scarcely be, or he would have made some effort to capture him. She therefore replied:

"I shall see my friends soon. I shall escape the first opportunity, you may be assured."

"Wontum knows that; but chief take good care of his prisoners. When comes to-morrow night we shall reach Pawnee village. *Then* Wild Bird shall either become chief's wife or his slave. Does Wild Bird care which?"

"You may not reach that place."

"I have no fears. I shall not leave the mountains at all,

but reach the cave by the rear of Independence Rock. Your soldiers are all mounted, and can not reach us, while we are in the mountains. An attempt to pass the Gate would be their sure destruction. So you see you have nothing to hope for ; and, if you are wise you will content yourself." The savage then pointed to the shelter, and continued in the Pawnee tongue :

"This will be your place to-night. But to prevent you from doing mischief, I shall tie both your hands and feet."

Later in the evening Wontnm bound the wrists of Manonie together with a thong. He then said :

"You used your teeth last night. I will prevent this." He placed his victim in a sitting posture, permitting her to rest against a large stone. He then placed a long strip of bark around her neck, and attached it to the body of one of the bent saplings, thus preventing her from moving forward. Another cord was then attached to her wrists, and her arms drawn forward, extending them at full length, where they were fastened. In this painful position the poor captive must remain through the long hours of the night, unless released by some kind and daring hand. Her child was placed near her.

Wontum stretched himself upon the ground directly across the entrance of the wigwam, but, for a long time, did not appear to sleep. At length his heavy breathing announced the fact that he was unconscious.

Manonie could not move. She wished to remove some of the twigs in order that she might gaze out upon the surrounding scenery, but was powerless. Seeing that her boy was awake, she *smiled* him to her side, and whispered to him to remove the leaves, which he readily and softly did. She now had a distinct view, but in one direction. The night was a lovely one. The moon was shining brightly, but the sky was full of white, fleecy, flying clouds. As the moon passed behind them, dark shadows were thrown upon the earth, assuming fantastic forms, now like the reflection of a stately oak walking over the bed of some lovely lake, now like some huge giant moving along, and again like the crouching, creeping panther, or the prowling bear.

Several times the poor girl fancied she saw the tall form of her unknown friend moving toward her, but the night-orb

raising the silvery vail from before its face, revealed the fact
that it was only a shadow.

Hist! What was that? She bent forward as far as it was
possible for her to do so. She could not be mistaken! There,
from behind a huge rock, a dark form emerged. It appeared
as if surveying the ground. It moved forward cautiously, and
then crouched close to the earth. Oh, with what eagerness
did Manonie watch its movements! Was this her stranger
friend? And was the hour of deliverance at hand?

Gradually the figure approached the outer row of savages.
It bent over one of their dusky forms. In a moment Manonie saw that a struggle was going on. The savage writhed
as if in agony; but gradually ceased, and all became quiet.
The captive then saw the stranger raise the form of the savage in his arms and disappear with him behind the rock again.
She kept her eyes fixed upon the spot, and it was not long
before a figure again appeared. But by the light of the moon
she could plainly see that the person bore the appearance and
wore the dress of an *Indian*. Still the figure moved forward
with great caution.

Slowly it moved over the bodies of the sleeping savages
toward the place where Manonie was confined. The form
moved to the front of the wigwam. The captive saw it. But
Wontum lay before the entrance. In a moment more a slight
rustle of the brush and leaves revealed the fact that some one
was removing them. The work was slowly performed.

At length part of the form, of what appeared to be an Indian, moved into the wigwam through the aperture it had
made, and, taking the captive by the shoulder, drew her toward him. This revealed the fact that she was tied. It was
but the work of an instant to cut the thongs. Then, in a low,
almost inaudible tone, the stranger whispered:

" Give me the child."

" Who are you?" asked Manonie.

" A friend. Give me the child, and then follow." As she
was about to raise little Harry from his earth-couch, Wontum
raised himself upon his elbow and looked around him. It
was evidently but the movement of one half asleep, for, in a
short time he sunk back, and remained motionless.

After a time Manonie carefully raised her little treasure, and handed it to the stranger. Then she followed him into the open air. She could scarcely breathe, so intense was her excitement. Oh, if they should be discovered now! Her bold friend would instantly become a victim. But they moved forward among the sleepers, and no one appeared to stir.

At length they had passed the circle. The rescuer moved forward more rapidly now, and Manonie followed with trembling steps.

Not a word was spoken until they had continued their journey for at least an hour. Manonie was the first to speak.

"Oh, how can I ever repay your noble conduct in venturing so much for me?" she said.

"I have ventured but little, madam," was the brief, but kind reply.

"Oh, yes. You might have been detected, and then the savages would have killed you."

"Very likely. But I have often ventured more in a cause not as good; besides, what is life to *me*, that I should fear to risk it?"

"Life is sweet indeed. To me, oh, how dear! I would that all were as happy in living, as I."

"I am happy in having saved you, and that I can restore yourself and child to your husband."

"May I ask to whom I owe so much?"

"Pardon me for saying it matters but little. We have never met before. I am simply a hunter, and, having learned that you had been captured, determined to follow and rescue you if possible. I think you are safe now."

"But are you not going away from the fort, instead of toward it?"

"Yes."

"I know you have good reasons for so doing; but may I ask what they are?"

"Certainly. The savages will discover your absence in a short time, though possibly not until morning. They will most naturally suppose that you will take to the valley, and make your way *toward* the fort. *They* will know of no reason *why* you should go in the opposite direction, and, probably, will not even take the trouble to hunt for our trail. But they will know that you had assistance."

" How will they know this ?"

" First, they will know that you never could have released yourself. And, in the next place, they will find the body of the Indian whom I strangled."

" I saw a form emerge from behind a rock, and struggle with one of the savages."

" It was myself you saw—the same who threw you the scrap of paper this morning, or, rather, yesterday morning, for it must now be after midnight."

" So I supposed. And you are *not* an Indian, although you wear the dress of one ?"

" No. I feared I might awaken some of the savages by passing over them, and I resolved to have an Indian dress. I knew if I could procure this, I might pass along unnoticed. Even if you were with me, the others would be likely to pay little attention to us, thinking me to be Wontum. I therefore approached the nearest sleeper, and fixed a firm grasp upon his throat. You saw the struggle. Well, when he was dead, I carried him behind the rock, and, removing his dress, put it upon myself."

" Was it your voice that spoke those words, ' You should have struck the blow ?' "

" It was."

" And where are we going now ?"

" I am going to convey you to the cabin of Old John, the hermit, as he is called."

" And where is that ?"

" It is at the junction of the Sweetwater and Platte rivers."

" Think you I will be safe there until my husband can be apprised of my situation, and come to my rescue ?"

" Your husband will probably reach that place before we do. It was the intention to set out with a body of troops for the Sweetwater, in order to intercept the band which had captured you."

" Then my husband does know into whose power I have fallen ?"

" Yes ; and expects to save you, and punish the villain who stole you away. Had we not better pause for a short time ?"

" Oh, no. With the prospect of meeting him, I never could grow weary. Let us rather quicken our pace, for I fear that wretched villain will miss me, and that he will find our trail, and start at once in pursuit. Oh, it would be dreadful if he should overtake us !"

They now continued their journey in silence, the stranger bearing the child tenderly in his arms. The sun was just rising when they began their descent of the mountain, and soon came upon a little cabin.

" This is where the hermit resides. Here you will be safe. You can precede me and enter."

Manonie advanced, with little Harry, and was met at the door by one she instantly recognized. It was Mary Oakley. Both herself and mother were lavish in their caresses, but, beholding Manonie's friend, they started back in fear. There was, however, an instant lighting up in the face of Mary. She bounded forward, exclaiming, as she sprung into the arms of the powerful man :

" Quindaro ! Quindaro ! Is it indeed you ! I am so happy !"

It was, indeed, that strange man who had rescued Manonie from a fate which, to her, appeared worse than death.

CHAPTER VIII.

THE PARADISE WON AND LOST.

MARY OAKLEY and her friend had not met for several months, and, of course, had much to say to each other. It would hardly be supposed that a man so stern in character, whose soul was brooding over past wrongs, and set upon avenging them; who was familiar with blood and scenes of terror, could find leisure to talk lovingly, even if he had a heart to love. But there were times when this daring man became almost a child.

Manonie, after she had reached the cabin and supposed safety, found that only excitement had sustained her ; and now that it had measurably passed, she sunk to the ground, quite exhausted. Mrs. Oakley assisted her to a couch, and, in short time, she was sleeping as sweetly as an infant, with little Harry nestling by her side.

Quindaro and Mary were seated upon the grass, under the shade of a large oak, and beside the beautiful spring of water already referred to. He had been explaining to her all the particulars connected with the rescue of Manonic, and his own adventures during the past few months.

" Oh, dear Walter—may I call you so ? It seems so distant and wanting in affection to address you as Quindaro."

" Call me Walter, dear, if it pleases you. I have heard the name of Quindaro as only connected with deeds of blood. I love to be called as I was when a child. No living being has addressed me as Walter since I lost my poor parents and my sister and brothers. And when I hear your voice, with its tones so sweet, and that name so spoken, it thrills my very soul. Oh, Mary ! how I wish my mission was accomplished ; that my revenge was complete ; that my oath had been fulfilled ! How I would love to retire from the terrible scenes through which I am doomed to pass, and, in some quiet vale, live with and for you only."

" And *can* you not do it, *dear* Walter ? Leave, oh, leave this horrid work for other hands. Surely you have earned rest and peace."

" No. There is one more who must fall before my hand ere I quit this truly accursed and unchristian life which it has been my sad fate to pursue for so many years."

" And that one is ?"

" Wontum. I have had a hundred opportunities to kill the monster within the past two days. But that poor woman and her child saved him."

" In what manner did *she* save him ?"

" She was his captive. I was bent upon her rescue. If I had fired upon the dog, it would have made known my presence. And I then could have done nothing for poor Manonic ; she would have been tomahawked on the spot. So I consented to forego my own revenge for her sake. Last night, when I crept to the wigwam where she was a prisoner, I came upon the Pawnee fiend. I drew my knife, and was about to drive it to his heart. But I refrained, fearing that he might be able to give an alarm. Had the other savages been aroused,

I might have killed others as well as that brute, it is true, but they would have prevented her escape and mine. And so, for the sake of Manonie, her child, and the husband who loves them both so dearly, I consented to spare him for a time. Besides, I would not kill him while he is asleep. Before he dies, he must know who it is that has followed him and his tribe so long, sending terror among them."

"And who is it? Pray, Walter, do tell me who you are—why you have thus pursued the Pawnees with bloody hands. I know it has been a just vengeance, or else you would not have wreaked it ; but has not the time come, my dear friend, when you can confide your secret to me ?"

"At some future time, and before we are married, you shall know all. In the mean time you must content yourself with what I can tell you, and trust to my honor and my love for the rest, dear Mary."

"I do trust you most implicitly, dear Walter, and it is this trust which gives a charm to my life, which renders even the mention of your name a blessing. You have created in me a new ambition. When I met you, I could not even read or write my own name. I feared you for a time, and then I began to admire you. I felt how inferior I was, and I began to put forth efforts to make myself more worthy of your regard and interest. I did not dream you would ever look upon me with eyes of love. Yet, how immeasurably dear you became. Admiration soon became adoration. I was only fully happy when you were near me. The time flew so rapidly that I could scarcely believe we had been an hour together, when, on each visit, you took your leave, telling me your stay had been for several hours ! Dear hours !—precious lessons ! Why can they not last ? Alas ! alas ! how selfish we are ! And still you must be my teacher—to lead me on and up. How I long to give language to the thoughts which, at times, almost *suffocate* me with their unspoken fullness. Ah, it is only the poet, I know, who utters these sacred thoughts. And that has made me long for their treasures. In the absence of books, I have tried to imagine what they would say *for me*, and the words came to me as if I was a poet—a made one, indeed, but still a poet ; and I have preserved them for you, not in vanity or pride, but to prove to you how well I have profited

your instructions, as well as how truly my heart is
ours."

"I am proud of you, Mary; and I shall feel repaid richly
my lessons have opened your heart and mind to the world
beauty, whose handmaiden is poetry. May I be permitted
see and read what you have written?"

"Certainly. Were they not written *for* you? They are
ours, as the words I would have uttered had you been near."

nd so saying, the artless maid produced, from her bosom, a
atly-folded sheet, which she presented, with perfect un-
serve, to her friend.

Quindaro opened out the missive, still warm with the glow
' that gentle nest from which it was drawn, and read:

> "The sun, how glorious and bright!
> Like its Divine Creator!
> To man the source of day and night—
> To earth the monitor of its flight—
> And life's sweet procurator.
> It glows and shines, how ceaselessly!
> It gives, and gives forever!
> And, like some home where angels be,
> Its glory ceaseth never.
> Beloved of my soul! I'd rather lose
> The light of that great glory
> Than that thy love should faint, or choose
> To wander where my eyes refuse
> To see *thee*, dear, before me.
> Thy love to me is life's great sun,
> Shining, how ceaselessly!
> By day, by night, it glows the same,
> By day, by night, it lights thy name—
> Ceaseless shall it be?
> Dear Lord, that rulest land and sea,
> Preserve for me, forever,
> The sun that glows for me, for me,
> And let it fail me, *never!*"

"Is it possible that you have composed this?" asked Quin-
aro, as he gazed upon the object of his love with his now un-
oncealed admiration glowing upon his fine face.

"I did, Walter. It was in my heart, and I wrote it out in
ords."

"It is the *soul* of poetry. I do not say, Mary, that it will
and the test of a rigid criticism, but that it contains the *true
ul* of poetry is quite certain. No one writes like that who
as not a pure soul and mind instinctive with God's best gift
—spiritual sensibility."

"Oh, Walter, how happy it makes me to hear you talk
us! I have learned the meaning of the word ambition. It

is a commendable desire to be great and good. And, if I fully appreciate the term, it seeks for great goodness; for, as I read in a book you gave me, none can be truly *great* without being truly good. By-the-by, Walter, I have never heard Father John speak of you, and yet I found that very book in his cabin only yesterday. I know it was the same, for I had marked it in different places. Do you know Father John?"

"The old hermit and myself have yet to meet for the first time."

"Then, why is it that I find *your* book upon *his* table?"

"He probably received it from your father."

"Oh, yes. I recollect now. My father *did* tell me that he lent the hermit some books. But, Walter, I wish you would see the old man. I am sure you would love him as I do."

"If I have had his character correctly represented to me, he is worthy of all regard. But you speak of ambition, Mary. Have you no desire to go into the great world where your ambition, if not fully gratified, could have a more congenial and unrestricted field?"

"I know but little of the world, and that little is only what I have gleaned from books. But it must be beautiful. I have read of the 'Garden of Eden,' where our first parents were so happy. And I have pictured to myself even a brighter scene, where *intellect* controls the actions of mankind. But there was a serpent in Eden. Is there any such where Christian men and women dwell?"

"There is an old adage, Mary, that there is 'no rose without its thorn.' Society is not free from such serpents as cursed the beautiful garden. Alas, that it is so! Where, upon the footstool of the Creator, can be found a place more lovely than that which surrounds us! Here is Nature fresh from God's hand. It combines, in its variety, much of the grandeur and beauty which the hand of an Infinite has vouchsafed to us on this globe. It is not even marred by art. Look around you. Do you see that broad valley stretching, far as the eye can reach, toward the eastern sky? See, the sun, as it appears over the mountain-peaks beyond, gives to each emerald blade a tinge of golden light, forming a picture which the hand of man could never copy, with all his skill. And look at the drops of dew, glittering and shining for a brief space, and then blushing, shrinking away before the rays of that glorious orb. And here are a thousand other beauties. The mountains, the streams, and ten thousand charms no tongue or pen can describe. Yet, all these beauties are marred by the presence of *savages ;* and *blood* stains the face of nature! There are many things in all parts of the world, whether in the crowded city or in the deep forest, to mar the loveliness which abounds on every hand. It appears as if the dark demon, which reigns within man's heart, must manifest itself everywhere—everywhere!"

"Walter, I do not think I should like to reside in the great, busy, thronged world."

"Would you prefer the dangers you are compelled to encounter here?"

"Walter, I am not so blind that I can not see that you are superior to myself. I sometimes think you would not love me if you had any other to love. If I should go with you into the society you have so often painted, I fear you would become its idol, and then you would forget poor, uneducated Mary Oakley. I would rather live and die here, because I can then enjoy your society, which I should be deprived of, to a great extent, if we were residing where others could monopolize your attentions. It is a selfish feeling, I know; but I can not help it. A *look* of yours might make a wound in my heart which nothing could heal."

"Why, Mary, I really believe you have become touched with the wand of the jealous angel."

"I don't know but I have, and yet I can not think it wrong."

"Do you know the derivation of the word *jealousy ?*"

"I can not say that I do fully."

"Jealousy infers *suspicion.* To be suspicious implies a doubt upon the part of the one suspecting of the one suspected. Do you think I am capable of acting a dishonorable part toward you ?"

"No. I believe in your truth. If jealousy means suspicion, I shall never feel its pangs toward you."

"Mary, look down in the valley."

The maid gazed away in the direction indicated.

" Look just beyond that rocky point, near the bend of the Sweetwater."

" I see. There are horsemen approaching."

" Yes. It is the husband of Manonie, and the soldiers from the fort. Oh! how happy am I that his wife and child are here, and will soon, be restored to him. It is unaccountable to me, and I suppose it is only natural sympathy, but every time I have heard that girl speak, it has thrilled me to the soul. It seems to me as if I had met her before, but it is only like a dream almost forgotten. But see. The soldiers are dashing forward at a rapid rate. No doubt Marshall expects to find his wife and child here. Well, let him come, for happiness awaits him."

" Shall I awake Manonie ?"

" Perhaps it would be best. I first thought I would permit him to approach and let his wife find him standing by her bedside when she awoke. But so sudden a joy might overcome her. Wake her, and let her see the approach of the party."

" Mary, your father is with the soldiers. Do you not wish to see him ?"

" Oh! yes. He will be here soon."

" He will be with us in half an hour."

At this moment Manonie came bounding forward, and exclaiming :

" Oh! look down in the valley. Our friends are coming. We shall all have such a happy meeting !"

These words had scarcely been uttered, when a number of savages sprung from concealment from behind the adjoining rocks. Quindaro was seized by a dozen powerful Indians, and despite his struggles—which were the most desperate— he was bound hand and foot. Poor Manonie was again a prisoner, as was also the friend who had risked so much for her rescue. Mary Oakley was also bound, but not so with her mother. Poor old Mrs. Oakley was stricken down by the relentless tomahawk, thus freeing her pure spirit and adding to that throng above another angel.

Wontum had discovered the escape of Manonie but a few hours after her departure, and, searching for the trail, contrary to the expectations of Quindaro, had started in pursuit. He reached the cabin of the hermit a short time after our friends had arrived. But there was a kind of superstitious awe which prevented the savage from advancing at once and seizing his victims. While the lovers were conversing together unconscious of danger, the eyes of the Pawnee were glaring upon them with the deadly hate of the rattlesnake. He recognized the terrible man who had so long sent death and terror among them. He knew he was the rescuer of Manonie, and that the savage found near the rock had been killed by his hand. He even wore his dress at that moment.

He also saw the troops in the valley as they were approaching. Now was the time for complete vengeance!

Wontum seated himself upon the ground by the side of his victims, and gazed upon them with a malignant smile. He then pointed to the troops and said:

"Ugh! White dogs. Your friends come. You want to go with them?

Quindaro made no reply. He saw that the savage meant mischief, and to irritate him would only be to render their situation more terrible. As for himself, he chafed like a caged tiger, but, for the sake of the females, he restrained himself.

He gazed upon Manonie. Her eyes were moist. But she clasped her boy closely to her heart, while her gaze was eagerly bent upon the valley and her friends. Still, she could hope for but little from these, as the Indian saw them, and certainly would not await their approach. Mary Oakley was almost frantic with grief. She sat beside the body of her murdered mother, sobbing and moaning. It was a scene to melt a heart of iron, but the savage only gloated over the wretchedness of those around him.

But he could not delay long. He, therefore, gave orders for an advance, and the daring Quindaro, Manonie, her child and Mary Oakley, bound and helpless, were forced along over the ragged mountains toward Devil's Gate, the stronghold of the Pawnees, and that, too, just as liberty and happiness appeared to be almost within their grasp.

3

CHAPTER IX.

TOO LATE.

THE heart of Lieutenant Marshall throbbed with joy as he gazed upon the noble band by which he was surrounded, and contemplated the mission upon which he was engaged—the rescue of his dear wife and child. He never before had felt the pangs of a personal anguish. His life had been one round of happy days—almost without a cloud. Since his marriage he had felt some uneasiness with regard to his wife and child, but had never dreamed that any personal harm could befall them, surrounded as they were by those ever ready to give even their lives in their defense.

When he found she *had* been captured, even in the fort, the blow was a heavy one. Indeed, it almost crushed the strong man. But, he rallied when he found it necessary to put forth personal effort for the recovery of his prize. He was now bent upon a daring enterprise. The object was sufficient to nerve the heart of any man. And he felt confidence in its success. So he dashed forward at a rapid rate.

Twice their guide, Oakley, fancied that he saw savages upon the Black Hills. A halt was made and a thorough search instituted. But, without avail; and this it was that resulted so unfortunately for Quindaro and his friends. Had these delays *not* have occurred, there would have been a happy reunion of loved ones. But, this was not to be.

" I see no signs of the savages," said Marshall, " and yet we are approaching the Sweetwater. Oh! my God! If we should not intercept them, what will be the result ?"

" Don't know, cap'n, but I reck'n we'll have some tall fightin' to do," answered Oakley.

" We will be compelled to attack them at the Gate, I suppose."

" Jes' so."

" And I fear such an attack would be fruitless."

"I thought soldiers had no fear!" replied Oakley, as he gazed into the eyes of Marshall.

"I have no personal fear. My fear is for them, and for these noble men who are with me. *I* would leap into the mouth of a cannon, if it became necessary, to rescue them. But I can not lead my men there. I must act in a rational manner. Each life here is valuable, and I must not permit my personal feelings to overbalance my judgment. I shall do all I can; but, when that is done, if any desperate adventure is required, I shall attempt it alone."

"No you won't, by a stockin' full!"

"What do you mean, Mr. Oakley?"

"Jack Oakley, I s'pose *you* mean. *I* mean just this. If *you* go among the Injuns, you don't go alone, by two stock-in's full."

"Who will prevent it?"

"A man just about my size; nothin' shorter."

"You'll prevent it?"

"Myself, and *no* mistake!"

"Oh, I understand. You purpose to share my danger. But, remember, Oakley, *you* have a wife and child. You should think of them."

"So I do, all the time. An' it's because I think of them that I feel so much for you. But they are safe up at old Father John's. Lord, if they wasn't, I don't know what I *should* do! I think I should go mad, if any thing should happen to wife an' Molly."

"Do you not fear for their safety during your absence?"

"Oh, bless you, no. A red would not go near Old John's."

"Why not?"

"They think he's a kind o' spiritual man. He's alers prayin', an' sich, an' the reds keep away. But, the old man is *some*, after all. Lord, he smashed my bones in a dozen pieces, t'other day."

"You didn't quarrel with him?"

"Oh, no. All in sport. I thought he was tryin' to bam-boozle me. An' so we just tried our strength, you know. Lord, but I *was* fooled! He chucked me about forty feet up in the air, an' I didn't think I weighed half so much, until I lit. Jimminy, I felt as if any one would have to take a fine tooth comb to scrape all my parts together. But, it is very strange we haven't heard any thing from him. You may just bet he's after Wontum, sharp."

"Did you not say that Quindaro was also upon the trail of the savages?"

"I did. An' between him an' the old man, I feel confident that things will be all right."

Poor Jack Oakley! He little dreamed that at that moment, his wife was but a few rods from him, cold in death; that his daughter was a prisoner in the hands of the relentless Wontum!

The troops had reached the foot of the hill. Marshall and Oakley dismounted and commenced its ascent.

"If they are here, it is strange they have not seen us," said Marshall. "From the cabin they have a full view of the valley."

"It *is* strange," replied Oakley, and a look of apprehension settled upon his face.

They reached the flat upon which the cabin stood. Oakley started back as his eyes fell upon the mangled form of his wife. For some moments he did not speak, but stood as one stricken dumb. Then a wild cry broke from his lips, and he fell across the body of his murdered wife. Marshall raised him up, but found that he was entirely insensible. However, by the application of water, which he dipped from the adjacent spring, he was finally restored to consciousness, but his wails were heart-rending.

When he had become in a measure calm, Marshall said:

"The savages have just left this place. This deed has just been committed, for the body is yet warm. So come, Oakley, arouse yourself. We have work yet to perform."

The old man started up and gazed around him. His manner had become more calm, but he called upon his daughter in an earnest manner. But there was no response. He then began to search around. After a time, he said:

"Marshall, the savages were over sixty in number. And Wontum was one of them. I know the mark of his foot. And either Quindaro or the old hermit was also here, for there is his track, fresh and clear."

"It is evidently so. But, can you distinguish the footprints of any female?"

"Distinctly. Here is that of my own child, Molly. Also another, small and delicate."

'Is there any thing that resembles that of a child?"

"Yes. Here is a small one, close to the door of the cabin."

"It is my boy, Harry," exclaimed Marshall, as he pressed his hand to his brow. "Which direction have they taken?"

"Over the mountain, toward Devil's Gate."

"We can not overtake them, for they must have had an hour's start, and our horses can not travel on these rough hills. Let us take to the valley at once, and make an attack upon the cave. That is our only course."

"And that is a dangerous one, although it must be tried."

Oakley and Marshall now returned to the spot where the troops were waiting. But their hearts were heavy. An explanation was soon given, and there was not a soldier present who did not clutch his sword and inwardly vow to be terribly revenged for the misery which the blood-stained human tigers had caused.

They crossed the Platte, and took their course up the valley of the Sweetwater. After a time they arrived at or near the Rocky Pass which was held by the savages. As the situation was such that a charge could not be made, Marshall paused to devise some means for a successful attack.

CHAPTER X.

THE MOUNTAIN WOLF'S DASH FOR LIBERTY.

POOR Manonic was unable to walk. The fatigue of the night before had been too much for her. And hope had become almost certainty. Even her husband was in sight. Now, how changed! But, she still had hope, and Mary Oakley cheered her with kind words. It appeared strange that this young girl could be so resolute; her manner did not indicate the slightest fear; she was even defiant, as it became Jack Oakley's daughter, and Quindaro's affianced.

A litter was formed to expedite her removal, upon which

Manonie was placed. As they progressed, she addressed her-self to Wontum, asking, in the Indian language:

" What are your intentions with regard to your prisoners ?'

" To make you my wife !" returned the savage, " and to take my revenge on that enemy of my race," scowling furiously at Quindaro.

" And Mary Oakley ?"

" Give her to the chief."

" And Quindaro ?"

" Burn ! *burn !* BURN !"

" You dare not burn him ! Such a crime would be retal-iated by the extermination of the entire Pawnee race."

" Ay, but I will. As soon as we reach the cave, I will show you a pleasant sight. He shall be roasted alive, even before old Nemona can interfere."

" Mouster !" hissed Manonie, with a shudder. She then cast a pitying glance at Quindaro. He was unmoved as if he had not understood the Indian's threat.

" You need not fear for me, Manonie," he said. " I shall find some plan to foil this villain yet."

" Did you understand what we were saying ?"

" Yes, the Pawnee language is familiar to me."

" But, I fear the wretch will put his threat into immediate execution. Do you think the troops can make a successful attack upon the Gate ?"

" We will hope for the best, at all events."

" What threats did Wontum make ?" asked Mary.

" That he would bu—"

" Hush !" Not a word.

" Oh ! don't be afraid to speak. Tell me the worst."

" Me tell," said Wontum. " Me burn white boy. *Roast* him ! Ugh !"

Mary gave the savage such a look that he actually started back. She then replied :

" You won't. Or if you do, it would be better for you that you had never been born." There was an earnestness in her tone which plainly indicated that she *meant* just what she said, whatever might be her ability to avenge the act.

" Ugh ! what would pale squaw do ? She only woman, an' woman only squaw !"

' I would kill you, you hideous villain. I would give your soul to the Evil Spirits to be forever tormented !"

The Indian laughed as if in derision. But, it was evident that he was not altogether free from fear, for he avoided her during the remainder of the journey, although the girl had no weapon so far as he could see. Her threat of *invisible* powers had filled him with misgivings.

It was nearly dark when the party arrived at Devil's Gate. They found much excitement prevailing. The Indians were ready for action, being concealed behind trees and rocks, and in the various caves along the narrow passage forming the " Gate." The troops which started up the valley had arrived, and already had commenced throwing solid shot and shrapnell among the rocks, but with little effect.

The savages were few in number. The arrival of Wontum and his warriors gave them fresh courage. There was a war going on at that time between the Pawnees and their natural enemy, the Sioux. This had but recently commenced, but it had drawn away from the mountain a large number of the Pawnee warriors. The chief, Nemona, had been detained at the Gate by sickness. He was anxious to negotiate a peace with the whites, in order to turn his entire attention to the Sioux; but, many of the braves, who had learned of the slaughter of their brethren at Laramie Peak, opposed this.

The arrival of Wontum only strengthened this feeling. He had started for the fort with two hundred warriors, and had returned with less than seventy. True, they had four prisoners, but not a single scalp. Some had been taken at Laramie, but they were lost in the fight which occurred soon after.

Darkness came on. The prisoners were placed in one of the caves and closely guarded. Soon the savages ascertained that Quindaro, or the " Mountain Devil," as they called him, was one of their captives. Their delight was great. They danced and sung, and yelled like madmen. They gathered around the cave where he was confined, and gazed curiously at the man who had been such a terror to them, and who had so long escaped capture.

A consultation was held. Manonie heard many of the words spoken, and turning to Quindaro, she said :

" Oh, my dear friend, I fear there is little hope for you'

"I hear their conversation, Manonie. But, I am not without hope. I think I can outwit them yet."

"What are they saying, Walter?" asked Mary Oakley.

"I suppose you will know soon. Perhaps 1 might as well tell you at once."

"Oh! tell me the worst, Walter, dear, do. I am prepared for what may come. *If you go, I go too!*"

"They have resolved to burn me alive."

"Oh! heaven help us," exclaimed the girl, as she clung to her lover. "But, perhaps our friends will make an assault in the morning, and we will be rescued. Let us hope so, at least."

"They will not wait until morning. They are gathering material now for the fire. Mary, can you break the cord which binds my hands?"

She made the attempt, but it was a fruitless one.

At this moment Wontum entered the cave followed by half a dozen powerful savages. The villain fixed his snake-like eyes upon Quindaro, and then said:

"Ugh! you kill Indian *much*. Must die now, like dog Must burn."

"I understand."

"*Burn!*"

"Yes. I heard your very interesting conversation with regard to me. As for myself, I have little to live for. Yes, Mary," he continued, as he saw the look of agony which settled upon the face of his beloved, "I understand your meaning, and I will confess that I have *much* to live for while you are with me. And I feel that we shall yet be free and happy."

Wontum pointed to a bright fire which had been blazing at the entrance of the cave; then to a large heap of light brushwood a short distance beyond. He added:

"Roast you here."

Quindaro comprehended his meaning. He was to be secured in the cave as in an oven, and literally roasted alive. The thought was a horrible one. But why was it material? If that rock was to be his tomb, would he not rest as sweetly there, after the death-pangs were over, as in any other place? Who would there be but Mary Oakley to drop a tear upon the lonely grave in the bright valley, even were he permitted to make it his body's last resting-place?

But what would be the fate of Mary? Would she be spared by the savages? What the fate of Manonic and her child? Would it not be worse than death? He felt sure *they* would not be compelled to share his fate. But the thought that they were to be left without even *his* protection, caused him a pang, although he felt confident of the ultimate success of the troops who were now before the Gate. Quindaro truly loved Mary Oakley, and his heart had already gone out in an unaccountable manner toward the young mother and her child. But, unless some unforeseen event transpired, an hour or two would decide his fate. A rescue, he could scarcely hope for. If he could only be free for a single moment, even though he was without weapons of any kind, he would make a most desperate effort to escape. The only hope, and this was scarcely a hope, was that, unseen by the savages, he might succeed in burning the green thongs which bound his wriss.

Another thought appeared to cross his mind at that moment. Turning to Wontum, he asked:

"What are you going to do with Manonic?"

"Make her Wontum's squaw!"

"And the child?"

"He brave. Make *good* warrior. Live with Ingens till get big."

"What are you going to do with the other pale maiden?"

"Give her to chief."

"Where is your chief?"

"There." Wontum indicated a position higher up the rocks.

"Tell the chief the prisoner wishes to see him."

"Ugh'! no! You must die now."

"Wontum is a snake—a coward. He *dare* not even show Quindaro the chief."

The savage started, drew his knife, and sprung forward toward Quindaro. But he paused as he saw his prisoner did not move. The fire was blazing so brightly that each could see the eyes of his enemy, and the savage would not have cared to encounter the bold man before him, had he been unbound. After gazing at each other for some time, Quindaro said:

"None *but* a coward would strike a prisoner; and that, too, when he is pinioned. If you are brave, unloose my hands."

"Wontum brave! Wontum no coward."

"Then unbind me."

"Ugh! No!"

"You fear me! You *dare* not set me free, even for a moment, although you are surrounded by your warriors. Your chief would not do this!"

Wontum turned to his men and gave some directions. In a moment four powerful savages entered the cave and seized the females, making a movement toward the open air, while others began to bring the brushwood nearer the fire.

Miss Oakley set up the most pitiful wails, as she struggled to reach her lover. But, it was of no avail. Manonic was more calm, but an agonized expression settled upon her face.

Old Nemona approached at this moment. He was accompanied by his wife. He looked upon Mary Oakley with something like pity in his expression, and then turned an angry gaze upon Wontum. The squaw, or chief's wife, who was called Topeka, (which term signifies "lovely island," or "beautiful gem,") approached Miss Oakley, and made an effort to comfort her but to no purpose, as she only struggled the more, and her shrieks became more heart-rending.

Even the chief did not appear to fully understand the matter. But it was all explained when his eyes fell upon Quindaro, and the preparations which were being made to burn some prisoner. Nemona was *not* a cruel man. On the contrary, he was quite generous for a savage. But, he knew Quindaro, and the injury he had inflicted upon his tribe. That is, he knew him as a mountain rover, and a terror to his warriors. He had considerable dread of him, which was not altogether unmingled with superstition. Still, he believed him to be human, while others declared there was much of the supernatural about the daring enemy of their race.

But, even this impression, which prevailed only among the most ignorant of the tribe, was dispelled to a great extent, upon meeting him face to face, bound and helpless.

"Burn?" asked Wontum, addressing the chief, and pointing toward Quindaro.

"Yes!" was the response.

At this the savages set up the most unearthly howlings, and began to dance in a frantic manner. They had so long feared the prisoner, that when they felt that they were about to be relieved of a terrible foe, their joy was supreme.

When quiet was comparatively restored, Quindaro said :

" Nemona is a great chief."

" Ugh ! Nemona is Pawnee, head chief."

" He does not fear, like a woman."

" No. Nemona fears nothing."

" Your prisoner is bound. He wishes to embrace his sisters before he dies. Will the chief release his hands ?"

" Ugh !"

" You see your prisoner has no weapon."

" Ugh !"

A large log was now brought into the cave and placed upon the ground. Quindaro was forced to sit upon it, and Wontum, as if to make his revenge the more complete, bandaged the eyes of his victim. The females were then forcibly dragged from the cave.

" Is the chief here ?" asked the captive.

" He is," was the reply.

" Do you hear the cries of the women ?"

" Ugh !"

" If you do not wish me to think you *are* a woman, you will release me until I can bid them farewell. If you *do* not, I shall think you fear me. Are you, with all your warriors, afraid of me, even if I am unbound ?"

" No !"

" Then show that you are not, by releasing my hands."

This appeal was to the *pride* of the savage, and *not* his humanity. Topeka also heard the words ; and, whether it was from sympathy and a desire to permit the victim to escape, or because *she* felt a pride that her husband should appear brave, as he really was, must be conjectured. At all events, she said :

" The chief does *not* fear. He will release Quindaro and permit him to embrace his friends before he dies."

As she spoke these words, she advanced and drew a glittering blade from her bosom, and severed the thongs. She then said :

" You are good. The pale-faces would call you *honorable*, *I love my husband and you must not harm him.*"

Quindaro did not for a moment comprehend the meaning of these words, nor did he afterward feel fully satisfied upon that

point.   If he interpreted them correctly, it was an unusual instance of trust.   But, after severing the cords, Topeka, either
by forgetfulness or design, dropped the knife before him!   He
covered it with his foot, at once.

Quindaro was astounded.   This had escaped the notice of
the savages.   He was sorry that she had done so.   It had
really deprived him of one-half his power, where it might
have been intended to increase it.   The chief was standing
directly before him, and must be the first one encountered.
He could not now injure him.   Had the knife *not* have been
left, he might have done so, but Topeka evidently had trusted
his honor, and she should not be deceived, even if his own
life was to be sacrificed in consequence.

The prisoner remained seated, pretending indifference.   The
chief wished to appear equally so, and turned away.

Topeka entered, leading Manonie and Miss Oakley.   They
both sprung to the side of the captive, and kneeling, sobbed
as if their hearts would break.

" Hush!"   whispered Quindaro.   " I must speak briefly.
Manonie, leave the cave at once; I am about to make a dash
for liberty."

She slowly raised herself, and was passing toward the entrance.   Mary had heard the words, and she clung to him,
while her sobs became less violent, and a kind of smile lighted
up her face.

" Oh, you will succeed?" she whispered, still not knowing
what means he was to use to secure his escape—so truly did
she rely upon his word.

" Can you keep your courage up until I can return with
the soldiers and rescue you?"

" Oh, yes; I can endure any thing if you are safe.   They
will not *kill* us, and while we live there is always hope."

" Then I will make the attempt *now*.   God bless you!"
Quindaro sprung to his feet.

Manonie had been watching him, and awaiting that movement.   The instant she saw that he was ready, she threw her
arms around the chief, and clung to him with all her strength,
at the same time exclaiming, in frantic tones:

" Oh, spare Quindaro! spare him, good Nemona—my Indian
father!"

The prisoner comprehended her intentions in an instant. The chief struggled to throw off Manonie, but did not succeed in releasing himself until it was too late.

Quindaro sprung, like a lion, past the spot. He struck at Wontum, but that wily and ever-ready savage avoided the blow, to a great extent. He was only slightly wounded.

The movement was so sudden that, before the warriors around were aware of it, he was outside the cave and beyond their immediate reach. Still, he was not yet free, as he well knew. He was at the upper end of the " Gate," and could not pass through that, as he would be compelled to encounter savages upon every hand. He could not pause an instant for reflection, as the pursuit had already commenced in earnest. Up the rugged hills he sprung, for among the rocks lay his only hope. He was but a few rods in the advance, and much of the time in plain view of his pursuers. He still wore the Indian costume, and darted among the warriors stationed higher up. These did not molest him, looking elsewhere, as they were, for the cause of the excitement, and thinking Quindaro one of their own tribe. This saved him.

Wontum was quite as fleet of foot as Quindaro. The latter was flying for life and liberty, while the former was urged on by his hatred and baffled revenge. He had sent a shot after his foe, but it was ineffectual. However, he finally succeeded in making those further up the mountain understand who it was that he was pursuing.

Quindaro at length reached an open space. Just beyond he saw a line, which plainly showed him that all escape, in *that* direction, was impossible. Behind him came his yelling, infuriated foes. Before him was a wall of rifles. To the right, an almost perpendicular precipice, and to the left, a mass of rugged rocks, and a thick, stunted undergrowth.

This latter was his most likely cover, and he darted in that direction. A dozen shots were sent after him, but he escaped any serious injury, by reason of running in a zig-zag course. This movement lessened his speed, and, when he sprung among the friendly rocks, his enemies were not a dozen rods behind him.

The passage became difficult; but it was equally so for pursuers and pursued. At length Quindaro came upon a ravine, which wound its way down toward the base of the hill. He judged, from its direction, that it must conuect with the Sweetwater below the Gate.

Hearing no sound to break the stillness of the night, he began to think the pursuit had been abandoned. He mounted the bank of the ravine and gazed toward the river. In the clear moonlight, he could see horsemen in the valley. They were not five huudred yards distant, and appeared to be working their way slowly up the mountain. A little to the front of this was a line of infantry, or dismounted cavalry.

While he stood thus partially exposed, he heard a sharp click near him, like the cocking of a rifle. Quick as thought, he sprung back into the ravine, and, with the same breath, the report came.

Another dusky form arose close by his side. A tomahawk whizzed past his head, but he escaped by a sudden "duck." It was evident *this* savage's piece was not loaded. He expected to feel the ball enter his flesh, but, instead of this, he heard the rapid steps of his foes in pursuit.

A little further on, he stumbled and fell. He was aware that he had encountered some human being. Quick as thought he sprung to his feet. Perhaps the dozen forms, which he saw, at a glance, prostrated upon the ground, were United States troops, awaiting in concealment, the savages. If so, he must quickly make himself known, or he would be dispatched, as he had not yet removed his Indian dress, which was worn over his other, and of course he would be mistaken for a savage. But should they be Indians in ambush, or watching those below, he must not speak too quickly, as his silence and dress might create confusion, and yet favor his escape.

But he soon became satisfied with regard to the character of those he had encountered, for they sprung up with wild yells. The unceremonious manner of Quindaro's approach, and the rifle-shot so near, apprised those laying in wait there, of some danger; but the appearance of an Indian confused them. Perhaps it was a Sioux spy! This, probably, was their impression, for Wontum, and some dozen others, who came rushing up at that instant, were received with a defiant war-whoop. But, before any blows had been struck, they recog-nized each other, and explanations were made.

Instant search was made for Quindaro, but he was nowhere to be found. He had taken advantage of the confusion, and slipped away unperceived. The mountain-wolf was free again! Wontum was almost frantic with rage. But he soon found something else to occupy his attention.

The yells of the savages and the report of the rifle had been heard by the troops near the river. The flash and the curling smoke assisted their aim. The booming of a cannon echoed over the hills, and a shot fell but a few feet from the spot where Wontum was standing. Another followed this, and then another. This would prevent all further search for the fugitive. So the savages withdrew to a safer place, while the baffled cut-throat sought out the presence of the old chief to report the escape of Quindaro, and, so far as he could judge by their movements, the intentions of the troops.

He found Nemona in a bad humor, and more than ever determined to treat for a peace with the commander of the Federal forces. But the opposition of his warriors was still very strong, owing, in a great extent, to the influence of the man whose personal plans were of more importance to himself than the shedding of blood, or friendly intercourse and trade between his tribe and the whites.

CHAPTER XI.

THE DAY BREAKING.

IN a few moments after the arrival of Wontum at the chief's quarters, and while a dispute, which amounted almost to a downright quarrel, was going on, a party of some dozen savages arrived, bringing in a prisoner. When this announcement was made, Wontum almost yelled with delight; but his face underwent an instant change, as he saw that it was an *old* man.

Miss Oakley saw him at the same time, and, springing forward, cried :

" Oh, Father John, are you, too, a prisoner ?"

It was indeed the old hermit, and he replied in a mild voice :

" No, my child, *not* a prisoner."

" Then why are you here ?"

" I came to effect the release of yourself, Manonie, as she is called, and her child."

" Release us !" cried both the captives, as they clung to the old man.

" Release *her* ?" asked Wontum, as he pointed to Manonie.

" I did not address *you*, sir," said the hermit, in a stern voice. " When I am through speaking with these poor captives, I will confer with Nemona, the chief."

This reply stung the wily Indian, who had no alternative, however, but to remain quiet.

" Did you see Quindaro ?" asked Mary, betraying her emotion in tears.

" He is safe."

" And my husband ?" chimed in Manonie.

" He is with the troops in the valley, and will soon be with you."

" You are spy !" yelled Wontum.

" Are you spy ?" asked the chief.

" No, I am neither warrior nor spy. My trade is not blood, but peace."

" Where were you taken ?"

" I was seized by your warriors in the ravine but a short distance from the river."

" What were you doing there ?"

" On my way to you to propose peace."

The face of the chief lighted up as he heard these words, but that of Wontum grew as black as midnight.

" What conditions," asked Nemona, " are you prepared to offer ?"

" That you cease all further depredations, release these captives, and give up Wontum for execution. He was the leader of this outbreak. You need not frown upon me so fiercely," he continued, addressing Wontum, " I am simply delivering my message. The chief can return just such an answer as pleases him. I will bear it faithfully. But I trust there will be no necessity for further bloodshed. You know I have always been a man of peace, Nemona, and I would counsel you for your good. You can not meet the white warriors, as they outnumber you, and have great guns to fight with. Let me return with the captives."

Topeka now came up. She took the old man by the hand, and gazed earnestly into his face, and then she asked:

' Are *you* Father John, the hermit?"

" So I am called, Topeka."

" The good old man whose wigwam is upon the mountain side by the Medicine Bow."

" My cabin is there."

" And do you live alone? Are you a hermit, with none to share your cabin—no one to love you?"

" I trust that there are some who love me. At least, I hope that I have not the enmity of any one."

" Oh, no. No one *could* be an enemy to you, and everybody loves you because you teach them of the Great Spirit. If they would all learn of you, I think we should have no wars. Will you teach me of that Being who rules in the sky?"

" Willingly, Topeka. He teaches us that we must not murder. Now, when some of your tribe were last at my cabin, they murdered a poor woman. It was the mother of Mary Oakley."

" Of that poor captive?"

" Yes."

" And has it left her no one to love?"

" Her father is yet alive."

" No one else?"

" Oh, yes," exclaimed Mary, with zealous simplicity, " there s one other. There is more than one. Father John is one and another is the one you—"

" Hush!" whispered the hermit.

" Oh, yes, I remember. The one who was in the cave. And do you love him?"

" I do," was the ready answer.

" As much as I love my husband, Nemona?"

" I think quite as much," she replied, smiling and blushing.

" Then you shall be sent to him. Who was it killed your mother?"

"I think it was Wontum," returned the hermit.

"You are a bad man," replied Topeka, in a sharp tone, as she turned upon the villain. "You shall be punished." Then turning to Manonie, she said:

"You did not love to live in the wigwam?"

"No, I did not, Topeka," was the reply. "It was not my home. It was the Indian's lodge, not the white man's house, and I am not an Indian."

"Well, you are a pale-face, and should live with them. And you could not love Wontum?"

"No," was the decided answer. "I would as soon think of loving a prairie-wolf."

"And I do not blame you, for he is a bad man. Who have *you* to love there?" She pointed toward the troop.

"I have a husband there, whom I love, and who is waiting for me and his child."

"Then you shall go to him."

"She shall not go," cried Wontum in an emphatic manner. And he drew his huge knife, as if to oppose any attempt to take her away.

"Stand back, Wontum," exclaimed the chief, in a determined voice. "I order here."

Wontum, while he feared to disobey, still had hope that he could divide the tribe, and that the largest portion of them would be for war. So he commenced a conversation, in a low tone, with the different groups standing around, which was either unheard or unheeded by the chief.

Topeka gazed earnestly upon Mary for some time, and then spoke, more as if giving utterance to her own thoughts, than addressing another:

"So that bad man murdered your poor mother!"

"Yes," replied Mary, as she clung to the breast of the old man, sobbing.

"How long ago?

"Only yesterday."

"Only yesterday? Let me see. It is fifteen years since that bad man killed—" She paused as if musing.

"Killed who?" asked the old hermit, exhibiting some emotion.

"Killed the mother of Manonie!"

The poor captive shuddered as she heard this announcement. The old man was still more excited, and he cried:

"What was the name? Where did she live?"

"I have forgotten," answered Topeka. "But my husband can tell you."

"Was *he* there?

"Where?"

"On the spot where this other murder was committed?"

"No," replied the chief. "I was at Willow Lake, and knew nothing of the occurrence until the return of Wontum. He brought Manonie with him. She was then a little child about three years of age."

"What was her name?"

"I never knew."

"Where was the place where the murder was committed?"

"It was in Iowa, near—"

This sentence was broken. A sharp rifle-crack was followed by the chief starting to his feet and placing his hand upon his head as if in pain. Then a crimson liquid oozed between his fingers, and he staggered and fell to the ground.

Topeka sprung forward with a wild shriek, and threw herself upon the body of her husband, calling loudly upon him to look up or speak to her. But he was silent. For some time she gave vent to the most pitiful moans, but at length she sprung to her feet.

Wontum and nearly a hundred Indians had gathered around and were gazing upon the chief. The wife confronted the villain with a drawn dagger, and exclaimed:

"*You* did that!"

"Ugh! Me! No!" exclaimed Wontum, evidently surprised at the accusation.

"Did he do it?" asked the frantic wife, turning to the hermit.

"I think not, Manonie. You see that the morning has dawned, and that it is quite light. Some of the soldiers have crept near enough to take a deadly aim, and have done this. But, let me see if Nemona is killed or badly hurt.' The old man bent over him, examined the hurt, and then said:

"Do not fear, Topeka. Your husband is not badly injured. The shot has struck the temple, cutting a slight gash, but has not broken the skull. He is merely rendered insensible by the blow, but will recover in a short time."

By the direction of Topeka the savages removed the chief into one of the caves where he would be safe from the shot which now began to fall round them very rapidly.

Now was the time for Wontum's triumph. The chief was insensible, and could not countermand his orders, and he knew the savages were willing to fight under him. And he thought they could withstand the assault a number of hours, even if they were defeated at all. So the conspirator assumed command, and the almost incessant cracking rifle and the war of musketry and field-pieces, told the story that the work had commenced in earnest.

Occasional yells were also heard, some of them speaking of defeat or success alternately. Many of the savages were concentrated near the place where our friends were standing, and it became very dangerous for them to remain. The old hermit saw that it would be still more dangerous to attempt to pass to their friends, as they would be seen by the savages; and if they, by any miracle, escaped the fire of their own troops, the Indians would shoot them down sooner than they should escape. This he felt sure Wontum would do.

He therefore led the females into the cave where the chief had been placed. Here they would be safe, unless Wontum, finding himself liable to be defeated, should enter and massacre them all. But this risk it was necessary for them to run.

The two captive females were in a state of terrible excitement. Oh! if their friends should be defeated! And now that liberty appeared so near, oh! if it should only be the *liberty of death!* And that, too, without even being permitted a parting word with their beloved ones!

Topeka was calm. She asked many questions in regard to the mode of life in the great world, and evinced much interest, but confessed that she had but little desire for change, unless her husband should prefer such a life, which was not probable.

Nemona had recovered so far as to be able to speak. His wife showed him every attention, manifesting the greatest tenderness and love. Upon a sudden, she caught Father John, and in a hurried manner said:

" Quick !   Conceal yourself behind me."

" Wontum is coming?"

" Yes."

" I will oppose him."

" Madman. He has a dozen powerful warriors with him, and they are all well armed, and you have nothing. You would be killed before you could utter two words."

"It is Manonie the villain is after."

" Yes."

" And shall I not defend her while I have life?   I will.'

"Then you can not help her now, or at any future time- .. Come." The wife of the chief drew the old man back, a..d screened him from sight.

At this moment Wontum entered the cave, followed by a party of fierce warriors, who were yelling in a frantic manner. Poor Manonie felt that she was the intended victim, and shrunk to the most obscure part of the cavern.   But, it was of no avail. She was dragged forth, while her shrieks filled the air with their echoes. In vain she called upon her husband for assistance. He was not there.

And yet once she thought she heard his voice ringing across the mountain ; still, she was not sure, as it was blended with a hundred others.

" My child!   My child!   Give me my boy !"   But the unfeeling monster heeded not her cries.

" Oh ! this is too much !" cried the old man, and springing from his concealment, he added :

" This is too cowardly."

He reached the entrance of the cave just in time to see Wontum place his captive upon a horse.   Then he felt a sharp pang, and fell back helpless and senseless to the ground.

" I knew this would be the result !" cried Topeka, as she sprung to his side.   " Rash old man—what could he think to accomplish against so many."

Miss Oakley had reached him at the same time.   There was blood upon his face, indeed it was covered, showing that the wound was there.

" Dear Topeka," said Mary, " your husband requires all your attentions. I will do all I can for poor old Father John, but I fear that will be but little."

"We shall have—or rather *you* will have assistance in a few moments. Don't you hear that the firing has nearly ceased? And see; just at the foot of the hill are the troops. Will they harm me or my husband?" asked the Indian wife, with much solicitude.

"No. Do not fear. You saved Quindaro, and would have saved ourselves. You shall ever be our friends."

Little Harry Marshall had been left behind in the cave, Wontum seeing that he had barely time to escape with Manonie.

CHAPTER XII.

REUNION.

AFTER the wife of poor old Jack Oakley had been placed in a temporary grave, the almost heart-broken husband followed Marshall until they had rejoined the troops in the valley. They then took their way up the Sweetwater. They were well satisfied that Devil's Gate would be the place decided upon by the savages as their stronghold. How many warriors they would be compelled to encounter was not known, but, it was supposed that at least two-thirds of their tribe had gone upon an incursion against the Sioux, whose head-quarters was near the junction of Pole creek and the south fork of the Platte river. Yet, even though their numbers were but small, they could hold the Gate against a large force, if they were determined so to do. As they neared the mountain fastness, Marshall asked:

"Oakley, do you not think that Nemona will yield without a fight, when he sees with what a force he will have to contend?'

"Wal, my 'pinion is, that he would never commenced fightin' ef it hadn't been for that villainous scoundrel, Wontum. I tell ye, cap'n, he's about the worst specimen of a red-skin that can be scart up in any of the Nebraska tribes. I thought thar' was some mean 'uns down among the Sioux, but this feller takes the rag clean off the bush, an' no mistake."

"Do you think it was Wontum who killed your poor wife?"

"I think it was. But what on earth he wanted to do that for, is more nor me can tell. Why, cap'n, she was the peaceablest critter you ever *did* see. An' she was a good Christian woman, too, an' that's some consolation. But I tell you, cap'n, for all that, it's left a big hole in this old heart, as can never be filled up."

"I appreciate your feelings, Mr. Oakley," said Marshall.

"Wal, perhaps you can, but I'll be blest if I can tell 'em myself. Why, cap'n, when I got up thar', an' my eyes fell on that form—that poor old woman what's been sich a true wife to me for more than twenty years, I felt jest as if my heart all at once stopped beatin', an' that my blood froze rite up in my veins. But what on earth did the villain want with my little Molly?"

"Is it not their custom to take captive every one they don't kill?"

"Not allers. When they go into an enemy's country, they generally do, but we've lived peaceably down by the Medicine Bow for a good many years, an' we never have given 'em any cause to meddle with us."

"Perhaps Wontum has ascertained that you went to the fort with me."

"Shouldn't wonder if he had. But I can't help it. I felt it was my duty to go, and when I *know* I have a duty before me, I'm going to try an' do it, whatever may be the upshot. An' I've got a big 'un before me now. I'm goin' to *kill* that Wontum."

"There are others who have an equal claim upon his life."

"Perhaps you think *you* have, cap'n ; but you must recollect that he hain't *killed* your wife an' child yet."

"I hope not !" said Marshall, with a shudder.

"Oh, he's got no call to do that."

"I know that, as long as he can *retain* her, alive. But, suppose we should make the attack, and it should prove successful ? Don't you think Wontum would kill her, rather than have her restored to me ?"

"I think not. He will attend to his own safety first."

"But he might kill his victims and then escape."

"No.   If he *don't* injure them, he will *only* be killed!   If he *does*, he will be *tortured*.   That will be some inducement. For he knows that he would be hunted the world over."

"Is it not strange that we have not seen Quindaro?"

"Wal, I think that *is* a little strange.   I am afraid he was taken prisoner the same time the wife was killed.   If this was so, Wontum wouldn't let him live two hours, and that would break Molly's heart.   But what is your plan of attack, cap'n?"

"I can not tell until I can learn something of the position the savages hold.   I think, however, I shall pass around Independence Rock, with a portion of our force, while we attack with our artillery in front.   I shall also place men on each flank to prevent the Indians from escaping.   Still, this will depend upon circumstances, and the number of the enemy."

"Wal, we'll have a chance to begin soon, for there is the Gate."

The troops now approached the stronghold.   The report of a rifle, and the wounding of one of the men, was sufficient evidence that the savages were prepared for them.   The artillery was at once brought into position, and a number of shot were thrown among the rocks.

But darkness was coming on, and the firing was kept up only at long intervals.   This was more for the purpose of deceiving the savages than otherwise, for, immediately after the dusk of evening, and before the moon was sufficiently high to afford much light, a party of fifty, under the command of a lieutenant, commenced a circuit of the rock in order to reach the upper end of the Gate.   As the way was a rough one, it was calculated that it would take the greater portion of the night to accomplish this.   Oakley accompanied the party as a guide.

The artillery was kept in position at the lower end of the Gate, and only sufficient men left to work the pieces.   The Indians have such a fear of "big guns," that they seldom attempt to charge them, therefore a "support" is, at most times, unnecessary.

The remainder of the troops were dismounted to act as infantry, and the horses picketed near the guns.   A body of fifty then commenced their ascent of the rock for the purpose of attacking in that direction, while Marshall, with a hundred good men, took his course across a point of the Medicine Bow ridge, for the purpose of reaching the center of the Gate. Daylight was the hour appointed for the general attack.

During the night, the fire was seen which had been prepared for Quindaro ; and, once or twice, Marshall had almost determined to pour a volley into the cave, which he could but indistinctly see. But then Manonie might be there, as well as his child and Miss Oakley, and he might injure them. This was his greatest dread.

The morning dawned. Marshall's men were concealed in the rocks close by the Sweetwater, ready for a movement. One of his men had fired a shot, and it was that which struck the chief. It was most unfortunate that it did so, as he would probably have prevented the fight and much blood would have been spared.

But the attack now commenced with fury. Marshall saw his wife and child upon the opposite side of the river. Oh, how wildly his heart throbbed ! And there was Mary Oakley, too, and the old hermit ! They were standing in a position of great danger. The commander was greatly relieved when he saw Father John lead them into the cave, where, at least, they would be safe from the shots of their own friends.

The men also saw their idol, the heroine of Laramie, and they only needed the command from Marshall to rush to the deadly encounter. It came.

"Forward, boys ! Forward !"

A terrific shout went up as the hundred daring hearts sprung into the shallow Sweetwater and dashed for the other side. Up the sharp cliffs they tore, as men bent on victory or death. They were met with many a deadly shot, and a number of soldiers fell, pierced with the fatal bullet. But they faltered not, and returned a shower of leaden hail quite as terrible.

"Cease firing !" cried Marshall, in frantic tones.

The cause of this order was apparent. It was just at this instant that Wontum entered the cave, dragging Manonie forth. If another shot was fired it might pierce the heart of his beloved wife. He expected to see her struck down upon the spot ; but, on the contrary, the savage mounted a horse, placing his victim before him, and dashed off toward the valley above the Gate.

"Quick! The way is rocky, and we can overtake him!" cried Marshall. "Don't fire, but upon him with your sabers." A dozen sprung after the villain, while the others engaged those who had not accompanied him. But that conflict was short, as a surrender was immediately ordered by Nemona, who, as soon as his senses returned, rushed from the cave to stay the conflict.

It may appear strange that a savage could mount a horse, and, with *such* a charge, ride swiftly and safely over danger-ous, rocky places. But there are many of the tribes who are said absolutely to "live" in the saddle, and have trained their horses to such an extent, that they can ride where a civilized being could scarcely walk.

Wontum passed the rough places, and struck into a ravine, which led into a valley. That once reached, he felt that he would be safe, for none of his enemies were mounted, and, when the way was clear, he could easily outstrip them.

But horsemen stood directly across his path, in large num-bers. Escape *that* way was now impossible. He cast his eyes behind him. On came the avenging husband and his friends. He looked up the side of the ravine. Here was his only chance. The passage was difficult, and he could not accomplish it with his burden. If he attempted it *without* her, would he not be riddled by the shots of his foes? No matter. It was *but* death, and that was certain on every other hand.

Quickly he threw himself from his horse, dragging Mano-nie with him. The husband was not twenty rods from them.

"I'll be revenged yet!" yelled the savage. He raised his knife over the poor captive, who now crouched at his feet, and, in a breath, it would have fallen.

"Fire!" cried Marshall. This order was obeyed, as the men saw that the Indian was in such a position they could reach him without danger of injury to Manonie.

At the very moment, however, of the discharge of the volley, a form darted from among the rocks close at hand, and dealt the savage a blow upon the head with the butt of his musket, which scattered his brains in every direction. The blood thirsty wretch fell to the earth without so much as a groan.

It was a fortunate interposition, as the shots fired, although they probably would have proved fatal, would still have given him time to strike the blow which must have forever parted husband and wife. But she was saved, and, with a wild cry, she bounded into her beloved's arms.

"But Oakley; let us look to him," exclaimed Marshall, after the first raptures of such a meeting had passed.

It was indeed Oakley who had stricken the blow.

"Oakley, are you much hurt?" asked Marshall, bending over the fallen hero.

"Wal, I reck'n not very bad; guess I'll stick it out."

"Our boys did not see you when they fired."

"Of course not. I came up so sudden like. An' reck'n it's lucky for poor Manonie that I did. Where's little Molly?"

"Safe at the cave, I think," answered Marshall.

"Shall I see her before I die—before I join my poor wife in another world?" groaned Oakley.

"Let us hope it is no death-wound."

"Wal, for Molly's sake, I'll hope not. I think I can stand half-a-dozen bullets any time; but, I should think, by the weight, there was more than that in me. An'—cap'n, has one on 'em struck my eye?"

"No. I see no mark. Why do you ask?"

"Cos it's kinder growin' dark all around."

"Can you endure it, to be carried to the cave?"

"Is my little Molly there?"

"Yes."

"Then take me to her."

A litter was soon formed, and the old man placed upon it. But, before he reached the cave, he had become insensible.

Mary saw the approach of her father, and, supposing him dead, her wails were pitiful, indeed. But Topeka examined his wounds, with her practiced hand and eye, and declared that, with care, he could be saved. After applying some restoratives, the old scout opened his eyes, and smiling, spoke, in feeble tones, to his child, showing that he recognized her. This filled her heart with hope, and, to some extent, she shared the happiness of those around her.

CHAPTER XIII.

CONCLUSION.

THERE was much of sorrow to mar this meeting. Many of the soldiers had fallen. Peace would now be restored, and the one who had been the principal cause of all the trouble, Wontum, had met a just retribution.

Nemona, the chief, had been ministering to the old hermit. When the party approached, Old John was sitting erect, but his face was so covered with blood, which had flowed from a wound on the top of his head, but which the chief had stanched, that not a feature was visible. Nemona was standing by his side, looking the image of fear. He held a strange-looking thing in his hand.

"What is the matter?" asked Marshall.

"Old man's scalp!" said the Indian, trembling, as he held up that which really did appear like the gray covering of the old hermit's head. A thought appeared to strike Marshall, and he said:

"Bring some water, and let me wash away this blood." This was done; and a pair of huge gray whiskers were removed.

"*Quindaro!*" cried a dozen voices.

It was, indeed, Quindaro—or, Father John, the hermit—one and the same person! Mary was not the last to discover this, and was not sparing in her caresses and words of endearment. Old Oakley had been watching, with much interest, and then he said:

"I knew the old hero was *your* father, or that you was *his* father. But it turns out that you are both *each other's fathers;* or else both are each other's sons!" A laugh followed this, and he added:

"It's kinder mixed up, any way; but I 'spect it's all right."

"And is it, indeed, my Walter?" exclaimed Mary, in rapture. "And you are not very badly hurt—and father will recover—oh! we will all be so happy!"

" Yes, it is your Walter, but *not* Quindaro."

" Not Quindaro !" echoed the friends.

" It is one whom you have known both as Quindaro and he hermit. Now, listen to me. Nemona, you were about to ell me where Manonie resided when Wontum slaughtered the amily and captured her."

" It was in Iowa, near Fort Des Moines, upon Raccoon river."

" Manonie," asked Walter, " have you no recollection of our early home ?"

" Yes, but it is quite indistinct. I recollect kind friends, nother, father, and little ones with whom I used to play—"

" By the side of the stream—"

" Yes—yes !" cried Manonie.

" Under a large willow !"

" Yes, I remember it !"

" And can you not recollect your name ?"

" Let me think. It was—" Manonie placed her hands to ier head, as if the gathering memories were mingling and orming into consistency and clearness.

" Was it Flor—"

" Florence—yes !" cried the now excited woman.

" Florence Mil—"

" Milburn—Florence Milburn—that was it. Oh ! tell me f you are not—"

" I am *not* Quindaro, but I *am* Walter Milburn, your own orother !"

———

" Come, come, Flora, for so I shall call you now," said Marshall, in a playful manner, " don't hug that man any longer, or I shall certainly be jealous."

" And I, too, exclaimed Mary, laughingly, though there were tears of joy standing in her eyes.

" Well, friends," said Walter, " this is indeed a happy meeting. But, it will be necessary for me to make an explanation It was a dark night, nearly fifteen years since, that the horrible deed was committed which deprived me of all I had in the world to love. I knew our parents were among the slain, and so confident was I that not a soul escaped but myself, that it never appeared necessary to search further. I followed the Pawnees, first to Willow Lake, and then to this point. I found that I must have some repose, and so I assumed the character and disguise of the old hermit. I was compelled to go to St. Louis for that scalp which Nemona has just taken from my head, and for the whiskers. I have often wondered why I was not detected, but I suppose the reason was, the characters were so entirely antagonistic—so singularly differ. ent, that I was not suspected."

"How did you manage to make your changes so suddenly?" asked Marshall.

"At the time I was in the mountain with Oakley and your- self, and never until now, did I wish my real character known And so I left you and made the change. I *always* carry my wig and whiskers in my bosom, unless I am wearing them. The change of clothing is done simply by turning my coat."

"But how did you manage the double character here?"

"I followed Manonie to the mountains, little dreaming that I was pursuing my own sister. I rescued her and brought her to my own cabin. There I was surprised and captured.

"Well," continued Walter, "after a hard run up the hill, I found myself almost surrounded, and escape impossible. So I threw off my Indian garments, donned my friendly wig and whiskers, turned my coat, and was then again captured, and brought into the stronghold, as a peacemaker. The remaining portion of the story you know. But now that the one who committed that horrible deed is dead, I shall henceforth cease my work of blood."

———

Our friends are all yet happy. Oakley recovered and re- sides with his children, upon the banks of the bright Des Moines—Walter, and Mary his wife. Marshall and Manonie could not be happier than they are with little Harry, their only born.

Thus ends this story, not too romantic for a romance, nor too strange for truth. QUINDARO and the HEROINE OF FORT LARAMIE are creatures not all coined of the imagination.

THE END.